"This was a mistake," Matthew said harshly, holding the horse's bridle. *"I don't want or need a woman in my life. I don't want or need* anyone *in my life."*

Lilly wanted to tell him she'd never seen *anyone* who needed as much as he did, but she knew this wasn't the time. His features were stony and grim, giving no hint of the softer, gentler man who'd just made love to her.

The scent of him still clinging to her skin, the taste of him still in her mouth, she mounted. "I'm sorry your father was a mean, hateful bastard, Matthew," she said. "But that doesn't mean *you* have to become one."

She rode away, but she'd gone only a short distance before she turned in the saddle and looked back.

Matthew stood in the shadows, staring after her. Never had she seen a man who looked so achingly alone.

Dear Reader,

Once again we invite you to enjoy six of the most exciting romances around, starting with Ruth Langan's *His Father's Son*. This is the last of THE LASSITER LAW, her miniseries about a family with a tradition of law enforcement, and it's a finale that will leave you looking forward to this bestselling author's next novel. Meanwhile, enjoy Cameron Lassiter's headlong tumble into love.

ROMANCING THE CROWN continues with *Virgin Seduction*, by award winner Kathleen Creighton. The missing prince is home at last—and just in time for the shotgun wedding between Cade Gallagher and Tamiri princess Leila Kamal. Carla Cassidy continues THE DELANEY HEIRS with Matthew's story, in *Out of Exile*, while Pamela Dalton spins a tale of a couple who are *Strategically Wed*. Sharon Mignerey returns with an emotional tale of a hero who is *Friend, Lover, Protector*, and Leann Harris wraps up the month with a match between *The Detective and the D.A.*

You won't want to miss a single one. And, of course, be sure to come back next month for more of the most exciting romances around—right here in Silhouette Intimate Moments.

Enjoy!

Leslie J. Wainger

Leslie J. Wainger
Executive Senior Editor

Please address questions and book requests to:
Silhouette Reader Service
U.S.: 3010 Walden Ave., P.O. Box 1325, Buffalo, NY 14269
Canadian: P.O. Box 609, Fort Erie, Ont. L2A 5X3

Out of Exile
CARLA CASSIDY

Silhouette®

INTIMATE MOMENTS™

Published by Silhouette Books

America's Publisher of Contemporary Romance

SILHOUETTE BOOKS

ISBN 0-373-27219-7

OUT OF EXILE

Copyright © 2002 by Carla Bracale

Visit Silhouette at www.eHarlequin.com

Printed in U.S.A.

Books by Carla Cassidy

CARLA CASSIDY

is an award-winning author who has written over thirty-five books for Silhouette. In 1995, she won Best Silhouette Romance from *Romantic Times* for *Anything for Danny*. In 1998, she also won a Career Achievement Award for Best Innovative Series from *Romantic Times*.

Carla believes the only thing better than curling up with a good book to read is sitting down at the computer with a good story to write. She's looking forward to writing many more and bringing hours of pleasure to readers.

Prologue

He stood in the shadows near the barn, staring at the big white house. At the moment only one light shone from the windows of the huge two-story home. He knew Matthew Delaney, the eldest of the Delaney heirs and the manager of this ranch, would be sitting in his study, where he'd sat every night for the past week.

But tomorrow the house would be ablaze with lights because *she* would be here. Euphoria cascaded through him and his heart raced so fast he feared it might beat right out of his chest.

Lilliana Marie Winstead. Lilly. Tomorrow she would arrive here. After all the time that had passed, after all the heartaches in his life, tomorrow he would be reunited with the woman who was his soul mate, his love…his very life.

He leaned back against the wooden side of the

barn and closed his eyes, a vision of Lilliana materializing inside his mind. The first vision his brain produced was one of her as a young woman. She'd been sixteen years old when he'd first seen her, when he had first recognized that she was his destiny.

At that time her hair had been a curtain of darkness that he'd wanted to climb into and hide in forever. Her eyes had been the deep blue of ocean depths and he'd wanted to dive in and die there.

But before he had been able to make her understand that she belonged to him, that they belonged together, she was gone. He'd been devastated, ripped apart.

And in the years following her disappearance, he'd searched for her, had even tried to take up with other women who looked like her. But in the end they had been terrible disappointments...pale imitations of the woman who was meant to be his.

A swell of rage rose inside him as he thought of those two women. He'd had such hopes for each of them, but they'd been nothing but stupid whores who had refused to understand their fate.

Now they understood. As they rotted in their shallow graves, he was certain they now understood. Just as Lilliana would eventually understand.

She belonged to him.

It had been sheer accident that he'd found her once again. He'd gone into a supermarket he never frequented for a pound of hamburger, and there she had been...pushing a basket just ahead of him.

He'd been so shocked, so utterly overwhelmed,

he'd left the store without the meat, but had sat in his truck and watched as, moments later, she'd left the store.

It had been fate, giving him a second chance. And now that he'd found her again he wasn't about to let her go. She would be here tomorrow and he would be here waiting for her.

He opened his eyes once again and stared at the big house. Matthew Delaney was hiring new help for the ranch and he intended to get hired on. He intended to be here to watch her...to wait...and eventually to claim her as his own for eternity.

He just hoped she didn't disappoint him like the others before her.

Chapter 1

Seventeen years.

It had been seventeen years since she'd been to this ranch. But as she drove beneath the wooden entry that proclaimed the area to be the Delaney Dude Ranch, it felt as if the years had fallen away and she was once again a teenager eagerly looking forward to visiting members of her new family and spending time on a real ranch.

"Maybe I should have called or written to let them know we were coming."

Lilliana Winstead shot a glance at the elderly woman in the passenger seat. "You didn't tell anyone that you were coming?"

Lilliana's adopted aunt, Clara, straightened in the seat. "I was going to, but it simply slipped my mind." The frown that momentarily danced across cherish the memories of a boy who'd been kind to her when she'd desperately needed kindness.

Lilliana. Lilly.

Matthew took a pitchfork and arranged a bed of fresh hay in one of the horse stalls. The last person he'd expected to see here was Lilliana Winstead. He hadn't thought about her for years, but there had been a time when he'd hardly been able to think of anything else.

Although he'd never had much use for his aunt Clara, the summer of his sixteenth year she'd brought her newly adopted daughter, Lilliana, here for a visit.

Those trips they'd made annually for three summers had been both eagerly anticipated and equally dreaded by Matthew, who would always be assigned the task of entertaining Lilly.

Spending endless hours with the beautiful Lilly had been a pleasure the likes of which Matthew had never known. Not only had her prettiness attracted him, but she'd had an infectious laugh, a sparkle in her eyes and an insatiable curiosity that had absolutely bewitched him.

"You show her a good time, boy, and keep her out of trouble," Adam Delaney would say to his son on the first day of their visit. "You make me proud or I swear I'll make you sorry."

Matthew shoved away the memory of his old man's words, but there was no way to push aside the anger that stirred inside him. It was a familiar conversation between Matthew and Lilly impossible.

Although it had been years since Lilly had been here, she knew her aunt had come to the ranch seven months ago when her brother and Matthew's father, Adam, had passed away. She also knew her aunt had stayed in touch through sporadic letters from Matthew's sister, Johnna.

Dinner was an awkward affair, and Lilly got the distinct impression that Matthew wasn't exactly thrilled by their impromptu appearance here.

Although he was courteous, it seemed a courtesy offered with a touch of reluctance. The shadows in his eyes that she'd once found fascinating now seemed even more deep and forbidding. She wondered what had happened in his life in the years since she'd last visited that had so deepened those shadows?

Not my problem, she reminded herself. But what made her slightly uncomfortable was that she had seen those same kinds of shadows in another's eyes not so long ago. And those shadows had led to a tragedy of mammoth proportions.

In that particular instance, Lilly had allowed herself to get too close, had allowed her natural defenses to drop, and the end result had been devastating.

She didn't intend to allow anyone that close again. All she wanted from Matthew Delaney was the assurance that Aunt Clara, the woman Lilly loved more than anyone in the world, could have a home here. Then Lilly would return to her life and anger, one that had become like a loyal friend because it was always there just under the surface.

He spread the last of the new hay, trying not to feel guilty about how quickly he'd left the table after dinner. Aunt Clara had indicated that she would do the cleanup, and Matthew had taken the opportunity to escape to the stables.

Seeing Lilly again had stirred myriad emotions and he felt as if he needed some time alone to put it all in the proper perspective.

He'd been looking forward to this time when the ranch would be dark, when there would be no guests demanding attention. No bitching, no whining, just peace and quiet, that's what he'd been looking for.

He needed time alone to figure out where he was headed, where the Delaney Dude Ranch was headed.

But in those summers when Lilly and Aunt Clara had visited, the one thing that had been conspicuously absent was peace and quiet.

"Hi."

He tightened his grip on the pitchfork as her low, melodic voice interrupted his thoughts. She stood just outside the stall where he'd been working.

"I'm sorry to bother you, Matthew, but I really need to talk to you." It was obvious she'd showered and changed clothes before coming in search of him. Gone was the wrinkled blue dress she'd been wearing, and in its place was a blue T-shirt and a pair of almost shockingly short shorts.

"Talk to me about what?" He leaned the pitchfork against the wall, then left the stall. As he stepped out, he could smell her, a fresh clean floral scent that eddied in the air. It was a scent that rang the chords of distant memories. He thought she'd worn the same fragrance years ago.

"About Aunt Clara."

Matthew frowned. "What about her?"

Lilly leaned back against the stable wall. The brevity of her shorts now gloriously displayed the legs that had been hidden beneath the long skirt earlier. Those legs looked just as silky, just as shapely as they had looked years ago.

"I'm not sure how to tell you this," she said, hedging.

A burst of irritation swept through Matthew at the realization that even after all the years that had passed, and all the beatings he'd endured because of her, he felt a stir of desire for her. "Just spit it out," he exclaimed. "I don't remember you ever having a problem verbalizing in the past."

Her eyes, eyes the color of cornflowers, widened at the sharpness of his tone. "She's lost everything—her house, her savings...all of her assets—through a series of bad investments."

"And so she's come here hoping we'll default on the terms of my father's will and she'll inherit the place?" he asked tersely.

"I know all about the terms of the will, that your father set it up so you all have to work here for a year before the ranch officially becomes yours. And I know if any one of you defaults on the conditions, the ranch goes to Aunt Clara."

She took a step toward him and placed her hand on his forearm. He suddenly remembered that about her forehead disappeared. ''But we're family, Lilly. I'm sure we'll be welcome here.''

Lilly hoped so. They had come a long way from Dallas to this ranch in Inferno, Arizona, and had been in the car for the better part of two days.

Lilly directed her attention back out the window. Years before when she had visited, the place hadn't been a dude ranch but merely a working ranch.

In the distance the huge two-story white house came into view, along with a plethora of outbuildings that hadn't been there before. Still, a small rush of happiness swept through her. Some of the best memories of her youth came from this place.

As they pulled closer, she spied two men standing near the weathered wooden corral and instantly she recognized one of them as Matthew Delaney.

Even though it had been seventeen years and his back was to them, she recognized his tall lanky length, the impossibly broad shoulders and the downward tilt of the black cowboy hat on his head.

Again a swell of pleasure filled her chest. Some of the best memories of her youth came from this man.

As the car drew closer, the two men turned, and Lilly felt a sense of satisfaction as she saw that indeed, the tall cowboy was Matthew. He said something to the cowhand next to him and the man nodded, then took off toward the barn.

Lilly parked the car as Matthew approached them.

''Lilly. Clara. What a surprise,'' he said as the two women got out of the car. He made no move to hug Lilly or kiss his aunt hello. Instead he stuck his hands in his pockets, his dark-gray eyes expressionless beneath the brim of his hat.

"We've come for a visit," Aunt Clara announced. "I meant to call, but it just slipped my mind." She frowned. "Lately it seems like lots of things keep slipping my mind."

"I hope we haven't come at a bad time," Lilly said, once again looking at the handsome man before her.

"Of course not," he replied after only a moment's hesitation. "It's been a long time." His gaze flickered over her, traveling from her face downward, then back up again.

Lilly fought the impulse to smooth a hand down the light-blue cotton dress that was wrinkled from the hours in the car. Instead she tucked a strand of her long, dark hair behind her ear. "Yes, it has been a long time."

There was a moment of awkward silence, one that Lilly remembered from years ago. The first time she and Clara had arrived here when Lilly had been sixteen years old, Adam Delaney, Matthew's father, had greeted them with the same lack of enthusiasm.

At that time Lilly had stood next to Aunt Clara, eyeing the four silent Delaney children with trepidation at the same time they had stared at her suspiciously.

"I was just about to head inside and get some dinner." He pulled his hands from his pockets. "Why don't I get your bags inside and get you settled in."

Lilly nodded and as Aunt Clara started for the

house, she popped open the car trunk to reveal two overnight bags. She handed one to Matthew and carried the other herself.

"Things are sure quiet around here," she observed as they walked from the car to the front porch. Although it was just a little before six, the sun was already starting its descent, riding low and transforming the blue sky with glorious warm colors.

She'd expected crowds of people. She'd expected children running amok as parents attempted to corral them, newlyweds oblivious to their surroundings and high-spirited vacationers.

"The ranch went dark a week ago," he explained. "We won't have any guests here for another three weeks." He opened the front door and gestured for his aunt and Lilly to precede him inside.

"Oh my, I can see I've come in the nick of time," Aunt Clara exclaimed as she ran a finger across the hall tree in the foyer. A light layer of dust filmed the golden oak beneath.

Matthew swept off his hat and hung it on one of the hooks near the door. "The housekeeper is on vacation for a couple of weeks."

"Then I can make myself useful here," Aunt Clara said, a satisfied smile moving her plump cheeks upward.

Matthew opened his mouth as if to protest, then apparently thought better of it. "Why don't I show you both to your rooms and you can freshen up while I rustle up some dinner."

It took only minutes for Matthew to show them

the rooms they'd used in the past when visiting, then he went back down the stairs.

Lilly was pleased to see that the room where she'd spent several weeks for three summers as a young woman had been left untouched in the passing of time. The wallpaper was perhaps a little less bright than it had been years ago and the bedspread appeared a bit frayed.

The bed was big and soft, and many a night she'd lain in it and dreamed girlish dreams about Matthew Delaney. She smiled now and moved to the window.

The view was magnificent. From this vantage point she could see the stables and, farther out, the pastureland that it must cost a fortune to maintain in this arid, desertlike climate.

She could hear her aunt in the next room, bustling about to unpack her suitcase. Lilly frowned. It disturbed her that Aunt Clara hadn't called to let Matthew know they were visiting; that meant she hadn't mentioned to him Clara's plans of moving in here permanently. It would be up to Lilly to relay this information to Matthew.

Matthew. He had been a young girl's dream. Because he'd been the same age as Lilly, he'd been assigned to entertain her those three summers she had visited.

She'd found him intensely handsome, heroically strong, and mysterious in a dark, poetic way. She had instantly developed an intense crush on him. And there had been times she'd thought her feelings for him might be reciprocated, but nothing had ever come from it.

her, that she'd been a toucher. "She doesn't want the ranch, Matthew. All she wants is a home here with the rest of her family."

What family? Matthew wanted to ask. The Delaneys had never been a family. They had been four children trapped in a life with a brutal dictator, four siblings who'd been isolated by fear and distrust. But Matthew didn't talk about such things. He never talked about it.

"Why doesn't she move in with you?" he asked, then realizing how cold he sounded, he hurriedly continued, "I mean, you're certainly much closer to her than any of my brothers and sister have been over the years."

She nodded, the gesture giving her thick, dark hair a sensual sway. "I told her I'd get a bigger apartment, that she was more than welcome to move in with me, but she insisted she wants to be here."

He fought the sigh of resignation that rose in his throat. "Then I guess she's going to be here."

Lilly offered him a wide smile that lit every feature on her face. He felt the warmth of that smile burrow deep in the pit of his stomach. "Thanks, Matthew. More than anything, I want her to be happy."

He shoved his hands in his pockets. "Did you really think I'd send her away?"

She grabbed a strand of her midnight hair and twirled it around her finger. "To be honest I didn't know what to expect. We haven't exactly stayed in touch, and I wasn't sure how you might react."

She was right. Many years had passed since

they'd spoken or had any contact. She had no idea what kind of man he'd become, just as he had little idea of the woman she'd become.

"How long are you going to be here?" he asked. "Hasn't school started in Dallas?" The last thing he'd heard was that she was a high school counselor.

"Yes, but I decided to take a year off." Her gaze slid away from his.

"Really? Why?"

She shrugged. "I just decided I needed a little break."

She walked over to one of the other stalls and reached out to pet the mare confined there.

Matthew watched her. He had a feeling there was more to the story, but told himself it was none of his business. She was none of his business.

Still, he had to admit to himself that she was as pretty as she'd been at sixteen…even prettier. She was still slender, but with curves in the right places. Her hair wasn't as long as it had been years ago, but it still framed her face with glossy darkness, a perfect foil for her startling blue eyes.

"You never married." It was a statement, not a question.

She turned to look at him once again. "Neither have you," she countered.

"That's right. And I never intend to marry." Matthew knew well the reasons why he would never bind himself to a woman. "I like living my life alone. What about you?"

She gave the horse a final pat. "For the most part I'm comfortable alone. I've never felt the need for marriage. I think there are just some people who aren't cut out for the institution.'' She grinned. ''And no, I'm not gay.''

He blinked in surprise. ''That didn't even cross my mind.''

''You'd be surprised how many men discover I'm thirty-five and never been married and just assume it must be because I'm gay, or at the very least highly dysfunctional in some way or another. There are times it gets quite irritating.''

He felt a grudging grin curve his mouth. Even as a young woman she'd been in touch with her emotions and had no problems verbalizing them. He'd always admired that about her.

''So how long are you planning on staying?'' he repeated as they headed for the stable door.

''A week, maybe two if that's all right with you. I'd like to see Aunt Clara settled in.'' She grinned, the infectious smile he remembered from their youth. ''But don't worry, Matthew. I'm a big girl now. I don't expect you to squire me around on this visit. I'm perfectly capable of entertaining myself.''

They both halted as the door to the stables opened and Jacob Tilley walked in. ''Jacob!'' Matthew said in surprise.

He hadn't seen Jacob since six months ago when Jacob's father, Walter Tilley had been sent away to prison.

''I'm sorry to interrupt, Matthew,'' Jacob said. ''One of your men told me you were out here and I was wondering if I could have a moment of your time.''

Matthew turned to Lilly. "Jacob, this is Lilliana Winstead."

"Yes, I remember you," Jacob said and held his hand out to her. "You used to visit in the summers."

"That's right," Lilly replied. "And you used to come with your father when he'd have a meeting with Adam." She shook his hand, then stepped back from them. "I'll just get out of here and give you two some privacy." Without a backward glance she left the stables.

"Pretty, isn't she?" Jacob observed when she had gone.

"She's all right. What can I do for you, Jacob?" Matthew asked, curious as to why this man would show his face around here.

"I hear the ranch is doing well," he said as he swept his hat from his head and fingered the brim. "Heard you're booked up solid through Christmas."

"We're doing all right," Matthew replied. He eyed the man patiently, knowing eventually he would get around to the reason for this visit.

Jacob shifted from one foot to the other, his gaze not meeting Matthew's. "This can be a tough town, an unforgiving town."

"Are you here on behalf of your father?" Matthew asked. Seven months before, Walter Tilley had been the executor of Adam Delaney's will and the family lawyer. Then it was discovered he was running illegal aliens through the ranch and was responsible for the death of a young woman who'd been working the ranch as a social director.

''No, I'm here on behalf of me...and my family.''
For the first time Jacob looked him square in the
eyes. ''I hear you're doing some hiring.''

''I always do this time of year,'' Matthew replied.
''I've got interviews set up for tomorrow.''

''I was afraid if I tried to set anything up with
you, you'd turn me down,'' Jacob replied. He
frowned. ''And of course, I wouldn't blame you if
you did. What my father did to you, to this ranch,
was inexcusable.''

''I've never blamed you for the choices your father made.'' God help him if anyone judged him by
his father's sins, Matthew thought.

''Then give me a job, Matthew.'' There was a
touch of undisguised desperation in Jacob's voice.
''I can't get anyone else in this town to even talk to
me about a job. Everyone knows what my father did.
Hell, my wife...my kids...we're all starving because I can't find work.''

Matthew knew the Tilleys had always been proud,
and he knew the emotional toll it must have cost
Jacob to come here this evening.

''Be here at dawn in the morning and plan on
working harder than you ever have in your life.''
Matthew hoped he hadn't just made a mistake.

Jacob held a hand out to him. ''Thanks. I promise
you won't regret it.''

After Jacob left the stables, Matthew remained for
a few minutes longer. He sank down on a bale of
hay, his thoughts going back to the conversation
with Lilly.

Funny, he'd always been surprised that she hadn't

married. He wasn't sure he'd ever met a woman who had no interest in getting married. Certainly most of the single women of Inferno had marriage on the mind, and there was nothing they'd like more than to snag the last available Delaney.

But Matthew's desire to remain single went deeper than a mere whim. He would never marry, because he was afraid he was his father's son. And as his father's son, he was desperately afraid that if he ever fell in love he would only manage to hurt the person most dear to his heart.

Better not to love than to repeat the sins of the father.

Chapter 2

Lilly left the stables and checked on Aunt Clara, who had retired to her room for the evening. Lilly fixed herself a glass of iced tea, then went back outside and sat on the wicker chair on the front porch.

The sun had disappeared and the purple haze of twilight was fading as stars began to appear as if by magic in the darkening skies.

She saw Jacob Tilley leave the stables and get into his pickup. She waved at him as he drove off, then looked expectantly toward the stable, assuming Matthew would soon follow.

When minutes passed and he didn't come out, she returned her gaze to the night sky. From her apartment in downtown Dallas she never saw the stars. But here they looked big enough, low enough, to reach out and grab.

She drew a deep breath, feeling more relaxed than

she had in months. The frantic tempo of the Dallas city life and the daily stresses of her job seemed very far away at the moment.

A week or two here and perhaps she'd be ready to go back and face her life...and her failure. She drew another breath, fighting against a wave of sadness so deep it sent a piercing ache through her.

She consciously forced her thoughts away from her job and instead found thoughts of Matthew intruding into her mind. As a boy he had fascinated her and she was surprised to discover some of that fascination remained.

As the years had passed and she'd remembered the crush she'd had on him, she'd always believed that she'd been acutely drawn to him due to the raging hormones of a teenager. But she was well past the age of teenage hormones and still she found herself physically drawn to him.

The moment they had pulled in and she had seen him, she'd experienced a slight quickening of her pulse, an acceleration of her heartbeats.

Nostalgia. Surely that's what she was experiencing. The nostalgia of that first crush, time spent with a handsome young man, the awakening of sexual awareness between two teenagers.

Hearing footsteps, she looked toward the stables to see the object of her thoughts approaching, his boots crunching on the gravel drive.

"Everything all right?" she asked as she saw the frown that deepened the lines on his face.

"I hope so." He lowered himself into the chair

next to hers. "I just hired Jacob Tilley and I'm hoping it's not a mistake."

"Why would it be a mistake?"

"Jacob Tilley's father, Walter, was our family lawyer at the time my father passed away. He's now in prison for running illegal aliens through our ranch and murdering a young woman who worked here as a social director. He also nearly killed my brother, Mark and his wife, April, when they stumbled on his operation."

Lilly gasped and listened as he told her the details of Jacob's father's crimes. "But surely you heard about all this," he said as he finished the story.

Lilly shook her head. "No, I didn't hear anything about it. But you have to understand, most of the information I get about the ranch and what's happening with your family is from Aunt Clara and the letters she gets from Johnna. Johnna doesn't write her very often, and I think Aunt Clara often forgets what she's been told in those letters."

"That's how I managed to keep up with your life over the years," he replied. "Johnna would mention a letter she'd received from Clara and Clara's letters were usually filled with tidbits about your life."

Lilly grinned. "They must have been pretty boring letters." She took a sip of her tea, then placed the glass on the porch next to her chair. "Whenever I visited out here, I thought you led the most exciting life I could ever imagine."

"Really?" She heard his disbelief in his low voice.

"If you'd been here longer than a week or two at

a time, you'd probably have realized just how unexciting ranch life can be. It's a hard life. It can be brutal.'' A hard edge had appeared in his tone.

He cleared his throat and stood. He moved to the porch railing and stared out at the encroaching darkness. For a long moment he was silent...a silence that invited no entry.

Lilly stared at the width of his rigid back and wondered if he dated, if he had a special somebody in his life. She remembered him as somebody who had difficulty opening himself to anyone, sharing pieces of himself.

In those summers when she had visited here, she had worked very hard to get through the barriers she sensed he'd erected to guard him from everyone. And when she'd felt she'd succeeded, it had been a sweet success.

But he wasn't sixteen or seventeen anymore, and she had no right to intrude on his thoughts, his emotions or his life.

''You mentioned that Clara wants to make her home here permanently,'' he said, finally breaking the silence. ''I need to warn you that there isn't any guarantee this place will be permanent.''

She looked at him in surprise. ''What do you mean?'' She rose from her chair and joined him at the railing.

He didn't look at her but continued to stare out at some indefinable point in the distance. ''I've received an offer from a development company that wants to buy this place in five months when it officially becomes ours.''

"But surely you aren't considering selling," Lilly protested. She placed a hand on his forearm, and when he turned to look at her, his eyes were as dark as the night that surrounded them.

"To be honest, I don't know what I'm considering."

"But what does the rest of your family say about selling?" Lilly asked. She dropped her hand from his arm, conscious that she was too aware of the firm muscles, the smooth skin beneath her fingertips.

He took several steps away from her and raked a hand through his hair. "I haven't told them about the offer yet. I've called a family meeting for tomorrow night and we'll all discuss it then. I just figured I should let you know that, at the moment, nothing here is permanent."

Lilly didn't know how to reply. She was stunned that there was even a possibility that the Delaney heirs would want to sell this place that was their roots, their heritage.

How she wished she had roots like this...a place that was home, had been home for years. But Lilly also knew she had no right to fight for a home that wasn't hers.

Again they stood in silence. Lilly tried to ignore the fact that she could smell his masculine scent, a pleasant combination of the outdoors, of leather and hay and spicy cologne.

She could feel his body heat, as if the sun had fevered him all day long and his skin still retained the warmth. Suddenly she remembered how much she'd wanted him to kiss her years ago.

There had been a time when she'd thought she might die if he kissed her, that a single kiss from him would have the power to make her expand and blow away with sheer happiness.

On those summer visits they had explored every inch of the Delaney ranch, he'd taken her into town for ice cream and to the movies. They'd even spent time dancing together at a Fourth of July celebration the town had put on.

They had indulged in the flirtatious games of teenagers just learning the power and strength of their own sexuality, but they had never kissed. Certainly she had wanted him to kiss her, and there were times she thought he'd come precariously close, but it had never happened.

She returned to her chair, finding it ludicrous that she was thirty-five years old and wondering how Matthew Delaney kissed.

"Did I mention that a moving van will be arriving first thing in the morning with the rest of Aunt Clara's things?" she asked in an attempt to school her errant thoughts.

"No." He released a sigh as if the very thought made him tired, and Lilly wished it weren't dark so she could see his face, see the expression that might be there.

"There isn't a whole lot. Mostly boxes of clothing and knickknacks, her favorite rocking chair and a few other small pieces of furniture. She sold most of her things in an estate sale last week."

He turned to face her, his features still shadowed by the night. "I'm going to be interviewing and hiring some new hands in the morning. Just have the movers unload the things in the living room, and I'll deal with it tomorrow afternoon. And now if you'll excuse me, I'm going to call it a night.'' He didn't wait for her reply, but opened the door and disappeared into the house.

''Good night, Matthew,'' she said softly, oddly disappointed by his abrupt departure.

He intrigued her. When they'd both been teenagers she'd sensed there was an unusual depth to him, a sensitivity that he tried to keep hidden from everyone, and she sensed those same things now.

She shook her head ruefully. Maybe she should call it a night, too. She'd done all the driving on the long trip from Dallas, and she was tired.

And apparently that overtiredness was filling her head with silly notions about a boy she'd once spent time with…a boy who'd grown into a man she didn't know at all.

Rising from the chair, she stretched her hands overhead to work out kinks that had tightened during the long hours in the car.

She froze with her hands over her head, a sudden, creepy feeling that she was being watched raising the hairs on the nape of her neck. Slowly she lowered her hands, the creepy feeling persisting.

Gazing around the area, she didn't see anyone around, although the darkness of night, especially around the barn and stables was profound.

Definitely overtired, she decided, and with one last look around she went inside and headed upstairs to bed.

* * *

The moving van arrived just after ten the next morning. Matthew was in the midst of showing around a couple of new ranch hands he'd just hired. They were standing near the corral when the van pulled in.

"It takes a lot to keep an operation like this running smoothly," Matthew said, trying to focus on the men before him instead of on Lilly, who had just appeared on the front step to meet the movers.

It would have been far easier to stay focused on the task at hand if Lilly hadn't been wearing another pair of those damnable short shorts.

"I expect each of my workers to give 100 percent at all times," he continued. In the bright yellow T-shirt, she looked like a ray of sunshine as she told the two men in the van where to put the items they'd begun unloading.

He focused back on the two men before him. "Any questions?"

"Yeah, is she your wife?" It was the younger of the two cowpokes that asked the question with a thumb pointed in Lilly's direction.

"No, she isn't my wife, but she's a guest at the ranch, and one of the cardinal rules of working here is that there is no fraternization between the guests and the help. I expect you to be friendly and helpful to the guests, but nothing more." Matthew looked at the two men. "Any other questions?"

"None from me," Ned Sayville, the older of the two said.

Eddie Creighton, the younger of the two shrugged his shoulders. "Just tell us what to do from here."

"There are a couple of stalls in the stables that need to be cleaned out and fresh hay laid down. Why don't you start there, and when that's done hunt me up and we'll get you going on something else."

He watched as the two headed for the stables. For the next couple of days they would be jacks of all trades until he could assess their strengths and see where they would best fit at the ranch.

Now the next problem he had to deal with was Lilly and Aunt Clara, and he wasn't particularly in the mood to deal with either.

He'd had a miserable night, his sleep interrupted by intense nightmares the likes of which he hadn't suffered for years. He knew Lilly's presence was partially responsible for the recurrence of the old, familiar nightmares.

She had no way of knowing the enormous price he'd paid for those special, seemingly carefree days he'd spent with her so long ago. And if he had his way, she would never know.

But the night of reliving the worst of his past had left him with a cauldron of emotions deep inside and he knew that what he needed more than anything was a little distance and some time to get under control.

With this thought in mind, instead of heading for the moving van and Lilly, Matthew headed for the stables. Within minutes he'd saddled up his horse,

Thunder, and took off, racing across the open pasture as if the hounds of hell were chasing him.

But it wasn't the hounds of hell...it was memories of his father. Damn Adam Delaney! Damn him to hell for having no soul, for scarring his children with mental and physical abuse.

Matthew dug his heels into Thunder's flanks. Thunder responded to his urgings and raced like the wind until Matthew reined her in, the fire in his belly dissipating to a more manageable level.

Seeing a fence post teetering precariously, he made a mental note to talk to his youngest brother, Luke about it. Luke took care of the fencing around the property, along with any carpentry work that needed to be done.

If they did sell the ranch, Luke would be all right. He was a skilled craftsman in woodworking and would never go hungry. Johnna, Matthew's sister, would be okay, too. Married to the local Methodist minister, Johnna also had a thriving law practice. They would survive fine without the yoke of the family ranch around their necks.

It was his brother Mark that worried Matthew. Not only was Mark's house built on the property, but his wife was expecting a new baby. Mark's life had been working with the horses on the ranch. That's all he'd ever done...all he'd ever wanted to do. If they sold the ranch, Mark would not only lose his livelihood but his house, as well.

Matthew didn't know what he wanted to do. There were days when he thought that if he had to stay here one more day he'd go mad. And other days when he absolutely positively couldn't imagine doing anything but what he was doing…managing the family dude ranch.

He rode for nearly an hour, the physical activity effectively banishing the anger provoked by the nightmares and haunting memories.

When he returned to the stables it was nearly noon and the moving van was gone. He unsaddled Thunder and brushed her down, then headed for the house.

He found Lilly and Clara in the living room surrounded by boxes, crates and the rest of the worldly possessions owned by Clara.

"Did everything arrive all right?" he asked.

Clara smiled. "Oh, yes. They did a fine job. I don't believe a single thing got broken or scuffed." Her smile faded and she gazed at Matthew with embarrassment. "I suppose Lilly told you that I'm an old fool and have managed to lose almost everything."

Instantly Lilly put her arm around the old woman. "You are not an old fool. You were simply vulnerable, and unsavory, slick people took advantage of you."

"What's done is done," Matthew said. "Now what we need to decide is where you'll be the happiest here."

Clara's hazel eyes peered at him curiously. "What do you mean? I just assumed I'd stay in the room upstairs."

"If you'd prefer, we could put you in one of the cottages. That way you could have all your personal things around you and your own space. It would be like having your own little home.''

It was a perfect setup. She could live rent-free in one of the cottages, and Matthew wouldn't have to share his home with her. He could remain alone, which is just how he liked it.

Clara's face lit up. ''Oh, but that would be wonderful,'' she exclaimed and clapped her chubby hands together. ''And of course I could pay you rent. I do get a little social security money each month.''

''That isn't necessary,'' Matthew replied. ''You're family and family doesn't pay rent.'' The words stuck in his throat despite the fact that Clara beamed him another broad smile.

''I'd like to see the cottage before we move her in there,'' Lilly said as she dropped her arm from Clara's shoulder.

''Fine. I can show it to you now,'' he said.

''While you two do that, I'll just go finish up lunch and we'll eat when you get back,'' Clara said. Before Matthew or Lilly could say anything else, Clara bustled from the room.

''Shall we go?'' Matthew asked.

Lilly nodded and together they left the house.

''The guest cottages are over there.'' He pointed to a row of neat little bungalows in the near distance. ''But I'm going to put her in one of the worker cottages around back.''

He cast Lilly a sideways glance. ''Are you afraid that I intend to put her in a shanty?''

Her smile held a touch of guilt. ''Not intentionally, but sometimes men aren't picky enough when it comes to living spaces.'' Her small smile fell aside. ''I just want her to be happy and comfortable. I feel guilty that I didn't know what was going on in her life, didn't realize she was getting into such trouble.''

''What exactly did happen?'' Matthew asked as they rounded the side of the main house.

The bungalows where several workers lived came into view. Although not as charming as the guest cottages, they were neatly painted and tidy.

''She met some man who talked her into investing everything she had in some bogus stock. He was obviously a con artist and she didn't even question his motives. He talked her into mortgaging her house and maxing out her credit cards. When I found out what had happened, we made a police report, but of course the man had taken all her cash and disappeared. He has yet to be found.''

Matthew gestured her toward the third bungalow and they stepped up on the tiny front porch. ''See? No shanty.''

She laughed, the sound deep-throated and intensely pleasant. ''Sorry for being skeptical, but as I said before, my main goal is to see Aunt Clara happy and comfortable. Can we go inside?''

He nodded and she turned the doorknob, and they stepped into the cottage. It was obvious she was quite devoted to Clara. Matthew had never heard her talk about her own parents.

The story he'd heard from his father years ago was that Clara had adopted some damn fool teenage kid whose parents had gotten themselves killed in a car accident. Adam had not been just skeptical about his sister's mental judgment, but contemptuous about the whole arrangement. He had not been able to understand why anyone would consciously make the choice to take in a teenager.

"It's small, but quite charming," Lilly said as her gaze swept around the small living room with its utilitarian kitchenette. The furnishings were plain— a sand-colored sofa and chair and a dinette table.

She opened a door to expose a small bathroom. The door next to it opened to the bedroom. The bedroom held a chest of drawers and a double bed. She went around the bed to the window, and Matthew followed her into the room.

"Not much of a view," she murmured more to herself than to him.

"But the price is right."

She twirled around to face him with one of her smiles that seemed to light up the room. "Yes, the price is definitely right, and I know she'll be happy here." She walked back to him and took his hand in hers. "Thank you, Matthew, for thinking about this. This is the best of both worlds. She'll have her privacy, the dignity of living alone and yet will have you close enough should she need help. It was wonderfully thoughtful of you."

It hadn't been thoughtful at all. A wave of guilt swept through Matthew at her words. It had been strictly a selfish gesture. He'd thought of putting Clara here simply for his own comfort, so he wouldn't have to put up with her day in and day out.

But he couldn't admit that to Lilly, not with the warmth of her hand around his, not with the scent of her enveloping him sweetly. He couldn't very well admit that he didn't particularly like the woman she so obviously loved.

He pulled his hand from hers, uncomfortable at the touch, by her very nearness and by the engaging light in her blue eyes. "We'd better get inside for lunch."

"When can we get her moved in here?" Lilly asked as they started back to the main house. "I'd like to see her all settled in before I leave here."

"As far as I'm concerned we can move her things in tomorrow afternoon and get her settled in then. The only thing I noticed that needs to be done is that the whole place could use a new coat of paint inside. I can get a couple of men on that immediately."

They reached the front of the house and he spied Eddie and Ned approaching. "As a matter of fact, I'll take care of it right now," he said, and gestured the men toward them.

"We were just looking for you, boss," Eddie said. "We finished in the stables and wondered what you want us to do now."

"Lilly, this is Eddie Creighton and Ned Sayville. They're going to be working here at the ranch. I just hired them on this morning," Matthew explained.

"Hi, it's nice to meet you both," she said, then pointed to a gold chain and charm that hung around

Ned's thick neck. "What a lovely necklace." The charm was a thick gold cross with twisted vines wrapped around it.

Ned reached up and touched the charm. "Thank you, ma'am. My mama bought it for me years ago."

Eddie frowned. "All my mama ever buys me is underwear two sizes too small."

They laughed, then Matthew told them about moving Clara into bungalow three. He told them where the paint was stored and what needed to be done.

"And could we move out the chair that's in there so Aunt Clara can put her rocking chair in its place?" Lilly asked.

Matthew nodded. "Move the chair into bungalow two."

The two men took off. "They seem nice," Lilly said.

"They're all right," Matthew replied as they entered the house. "Neither of them has much ranch experience, but both seemed eager to learn and promised to be hard workers."

"What about Jacob? Did he show up this morning?"

"At dawn. I sent him out to the old barn that we're getting ready to renovate. The plans are to turn it into sort of a community building. Mark has been working on getting it cleaned up."

Abby raised one of her dark eyebrows. "Lots of hiring and renovating going on for something you aren't sure is permanent," she observed.

"Ah, there you are and just in time," Clara

greeted them as they walked into the kitchen. "I've just put it all on the table."

"You didn't have to do this," Matthew protested as they took their places at the table. "You aren't responsible for the meals around here."

"But I wanted to," Clara exclaimed. She leaned over and patted Matthew on the shoulder. "If I can't do for my family, then what good am I?"

Matthew said nothing. If she'd wanted to do for her family, she should have done something years ago. She should have done something to save him and his brothers and sister from their father.

Anything she did for them now was too little, too late. And for that he could never forgive her.

Chapter 3

The afternoon stretched out before Lilly. Matthew disappeared immediately after lunch, telling them he had chores to attend to. Lilly thought about tagging along as she had when he'd done his chores on those long-ago summer days. However, something about his closed-off expression forbade her to follow him.

"I just knew things would be fine here," Aunt Clara said as the two women cleared the lunch dishes from the table. "And it's wonderful I'm going to have my own little place."

"And it's a nice little cottage," Lilly assured her. "Small, but quite nice."

"Small is fine, with it just being me." She filled the sink with soapy water to wash the few dishes they had used. "When you come to visit, you can either sleep on my sofa in the cottage or stay here. And you will visit frequently, won't you?"

Lilly smiled assuredly. "Of course. When I get back to work, I'll have Christmas and spring vacations and all summer long to visit you."

Aunt Clara nodded in satisfaction and plunged the glassware into the sink water. "Of course, what would really be nice is if you'd move here to Inferno. They have schools here, and I'm sure they would be thrilled to get a skilled and caring counselor like you."

Lilly laughed. "One step at a time, Aunt Clara. At the moment my main concern is seeing you settled in."

Aunt Clara frowned and handed Lilly a soapy glass to rinse and dry. "I can't believe I let that young man talk me into mortgaging my home and giving him all my money. He seemed like such a nice young man, too." She pulled her hands from the soapy water, grabbed a towel and sank down at the table.

"I guess the saying is true, there's no fool like an old fool." She closed her eyes and sat perfectly silent for a moment.

"Aunt Clara, are you all right?" Lilly dried her hands and knelt down next to the older woman, who suddenly appeared deathly pale.

"Fine, fine. I just got a little dizzy spell." She looked at Lilly in bewilderment. "Now what were we talking about?"

"We were talking about the fact that I think we need to get you in for a checkup with a doctor," Lilly said, worry fluttering through her.

"Nonsense," Aunt Clara exclaimed and stood.

"I'm fit as a fiddle, I just sometimes move a little too fast or something."

The two women returned to the sink, where they washed and dried the dishes and chattered about inconsequential things.

When they had finished putting the dishes away, Lilly asked if Clara would like to take a walk with her.

Clara declined, stating that perhaps she would take a little nap so she'd be rested for the family meeting that night. "It will be so nice to see everyone this evening. Did you know Mark has a nine-year-old stepson, and Luke is the stepfather to a precious little girl and boy. So many new family members, such joy. You are coming to the meeting?"

"Oh, I don't know," Lilly said hesitantly. "I might pop my head in to say hello to everyone, but I don't think it's a good idea...."

"Nonsense," Clara said. She reached up and placed her hands on Lilly's cheeks. It was a gesture as familiar to Lilly as her own heartbeat. "Legally your last name might be Winstead, but in your heart, and in my heart, you're a Delaney through and through. And you should be at that family meeting."

Lilly smiled and pulled Clara's hands from her cheeks. She planted a kiss in each hand, then closed Clara's fingers as if to capture the kisses. "We'll see and now I think I'll take a little walk. Sure you won't join me?"

"Not me, but enjoy the sunshine."

Sunshine. There was plenty of that in Inferno, Arizona, Lilly thought as she stepped out the front door a few minutes later.

Although it was October, the sunshine was bright and warm and the temperature was in the eighties. Lilly had no specific destination or direction in mind, but she set off walking in the direction of the old barn Matthew had mentioned they were renovating.

Lilly and Matthew had spent lots of time in that barn years ago. Back then the barn had been in use, the loft filled with bales of hay, the lower level storage for machinery and grain.

The two teenagers would crawl up in the loft, make themselves comfortable among the hay, and talk. Well, actually, Lilly would do most of the talking.

Thinking back, it was funny to realize that she'd never shared with him the circumstances of his aunt "adopting" her, and he'd never spoken about his family. It was as if they'd both silently agreed that discussing parents or personal history was off-limits.

Instead they spoke of school and favorite subjects, they discussed and compared ranch life and city life. They shared dreams and talked about what they saw for themselves in the future. But always Lilly sensed turbulent emotions just beneath his surface, simmering passions that he kept tightly reined.

Brush tickled her ankles as she walked, and the heat on her shoulders was pleasant. Although much of the Delaney ranch was desert-like, there was a beauty in the landscape that surrounded her.

To the distant right of where she walked, she

could see the green grass and tall trees she knew were nourished by a nearby creek. She and Matthew had waded in the creek numerous times. She could still remember how he'd looked with his jeans rolled up to expose his athletic calves and his shirtless chest so broad and tanned.

She shook her head to dispel the images from the past. Oh, that boy had stirred frightening, wonderful yearnings inside her teenage heart. And it unsettled her more than a little that the adult Matthew seemed to be stirring the same kinds of feelings in an adult Lilliana Winstead.

The old barn rose up in the distance. Weathered gray and minus the doors, the place certainly wasn't the one from her memory. Just as Matthew wasn't the young boy of my memories, she reminded herself.

As she walked closer, she saw Mark, Matthew's brother, and Jacob Tilley carrying out a load of old lumber and dumping it into the bed of a pickup.

"Lilly." Mark swept his hat off his head and approached her with a friendly smile. "Matthew told me this morning that you and Aunt Clara had come to visit."

"Yes, I'm visiting, but Aunt Clara is planning on staying," she replied. "And I understand congratulations are in order for you. Not only a new wife and stepson, but also a baby on the way. Congratulations, Mark."

His likable features radiated with the brightness of his smile. "Yeah, pretty amazing. I didn't think any of us would ever marry or have families, and suddenly we're all the marrying sort.''

''Except Matthew,'' she said.

His smile turned rueful. ''Yeah, except Matthew. Matthew doesn't date…he dictates.'' Shadows fell into Mark's eyes, as if thoughts of his older brother saddened him. ''I think maybe Matthew feels safest alone.''

Lilly desperately wanted to ask more questions, to explore what Mark meant by his words, but at that moment Jacob joined them. He asked Mark about what to do with additional items in the barn.

''I hate to cut our reunion short, but we've got a load of lumber arriving first thing in the morning and need to get the rest of this work done,'' Mark said.

''Please, don't let me interrupt you,'' Lilly exclaimed. ''I was just doing a little walking to stretch my legs.''

''You'll be at the family meeting tonight?''

Lilly shrugged. ''Probably.''

''Nice seeing you again,'' Jacob said as he and Mark headed back to the barn. Lilly watched until the two men had disappeared into the barn, then turned and headed toward the house.

Matthew feels safest alone.

An interesting statement, and she wondered exactly what Mark had meant by his words about his brother.

Before going back to the house, Lilly stopped in at cottage three to see how the painting was coming along. She found Ned and Eddie at work in the living room. They both offered her friendly smiles.

"We'll have this place knocked out and looking just fine for your aunt by this evening," Ned said, a friendly smile curving his thin lips upward.

"We already gave the bedroom a nice new coat," Eddie added.

"I appreciate it," she replied. "It all looks very nice. Do you two stay here on the ranch?" she asked.

"Not me," Ned said. "I rent a small house in town. I like to separate my work life from my private life."

"And I rent an old shed that's been renovated into a little cabin at the Watson ranch down the road a piece," Eddie explained.

Realizing she was keeping them away from their work, she murmured a goodbye then went back to the main house. Once there, she went into the kitchen, poured herself a glass of iced tea, then returned to the porch, where the chairs were in the shade.

Matthew feels safest alone.

Again Mark's words played around and around in Lilly's head. Oddly enough, she understood. Oh, she didn't understand what emotional barriers might be in play inside Matthew. But she certainly understood the choice to live a life alone to keep oneself emotionally intact. Wasn't that exactly what she had done?

Sure, she'd had relationships with men in the past, but when they got too close, when she feared becoming vulnerable, she walked away. She would never put herself in a position again where somebody important in her life would walk away from her.

Safer to be alone. Yes, she knew all about that. What she didn't know was what had caused Matthew to make the same decision about himself.

From the master bedroom downstairs in the back of the house, Matthew heard his brothers and sister and in-laws arriving for the family meeting.

The sounds of their laughter, the easiness that had grown between them over the past couple of months emphasized an isolation Matthew hadn't realized he felt until this moment.

He stared at his reflection in the dresser mirror, a deep frown creasing his forehead as the laughter and merriment seeped in through his closed bedroom door.

Of course they had found a new camaraderie, because they were all newlyweds, full of the bliss of family life. And that was fine for them, but it was certainly a club he didn't intend to join.

For just a moment, as he looked at himself, he thought he saw his father's visage glaring back at him. He shook his head and forced his lips into a smile, an expression his father had rarely worn. The ghost image disappeared, and with a grunt of satisfaction Matthew left the bedroom.

The family was gathered in the living room, having successfully maneuvered the obstacle course just inside the room of Aunt Clara's boxes and belongings.

Luke and his wife, Abby, sat on the sofa; Johnna and her husband, Jerrod, were next to them. Mark and April sat on the love seat, and Lilly and Clara were in wing chairs.

Lilly looked as pretty as a picture against the wine-colored high-backed chair. She'd done something different to her hair. It didn't hang loose but rather was twisted in some sort of bun at her nape, exposing the long, graceful curve of her neck.

She wore a pale-pink cotton dress, short enough to expose bare legs and white sandals that displayed toenails painted a feminine pink.

She smiled at him as he entered, and the smile held the heat of a warm, summer day. Tension filled him in response. He didn't want to find her attractive, didn't want to feel the magnetic pull of desire for her.

The group fell silent as Matthew walked to stand in front of the fireplace facing them all. "Where are the children?" he asked, referring to Mark and Johnna's son, Brian, and Luke and Abby's son, Jason, and daughter, Jessica.

"Brian took them outside to play," Mark said.

"And doll babies they are, all three of them," Clara beamed. "And another baby on the way." She smiled at April, who grinned back and touched the palm of her hand to her stomach. "So much happiness in this family."

Matthew frowned. "Let's get started here," he

said. "I called this meeting because we have business to attend to."

"Well, we know you didn't call it because you just wanted to see and visit with us all," Johnna said dryly.

"Johnna, don't start," Mark said softly.

"I'm not starting anything," Johnna protested.

"Is there anything anyone would like to bring up before I discuss the reason I called the meeting?" Matthew ignored his sister, who always seemed to take great pleasure in needling him.

"I'd like to discuss something," April said. She stood, a pretty blonde with green eyes, who had captured Mark's heart when she'd come here seven months ago to work as a social director. "I'd like to plan a Halloween party."

"But we don't have any guests for Halloween. We're still dark that night," Matthew said. "Guests don't start arriving again until November 2."

"I don't want the party to be for guests, but rather for the workers." She offered him a tentative smile. "I'd like to do a real costume party, with candy for the kids and games and all kinds of fun. I think it would be really good for morale."

"We aren't here to boost morale. We're here to run a dude ranch," he replied, sounding stiff and unyielding to his own ears.

"Personally, I think it's a wonderful idea," Johnna exclaimed. "Honestly, Matthew, why don't you loosen up a little. Things have been rough around here lately, and happy workers make productive workers."

Several of the others voiced their agreement and enthusiasm for such a party. "Fine," he finally capitulated. "If you all want to have a party, then have it. You deal with it, I've got plenty of other things to deal with around here."

"So what did you want to discuss?" Mark asked.

"I got a call the other day from Dale Maxwell, president of Maxwell Redevelopment, a company based in Phoenix. He made us an offer to buy this place once the terms of the will are met and we take official ownership."

Mark leaned forward. "I hope you told him to go to hell."

"I told him I needed to discuss the offer with all of you."

"I've heard of Maxwell Redevelopment, they're into building time-share properties," Luke said.

"The offer was a generous one," Matthew said, and named the figure the company had thrown out to him.

"When we first learned the terms of Father's will, I was one of the ones who yelled the loudest about having to spend time here, working once again for the family ranch," Johnna said. "But, now, after spending the past seven months working here again, I'm not sure I'm willing to just sell out."

"I agree," Luke replied.

Matthew felt an invisible constricting band tightening up around his chest. He hadn't realized until this moment that he'd half hoped they would all vote to sell the place. "But, if we sell, we can take the money and build new lives." And they wouldn't have to pretend anymore that they were a real, functioning family.

"Could I say something?" Clara asked with a tentative smile. "I know I have no right to be part of a vote or anything," she began. "But I would hate to see you all sell this land. My parents settled here before you all and their parents before them. This isn't just a ranch, it's your roots, your heritage, and your father spent his blood and tears building it into something grand."

She knew nothing about his father, Matthew thought irritably. It wasn't Adam Delaney's blood and tears that had built this place. It had been the blood and tears of his children, whom he'd used like slave labor.

"Personally, I don't intend to sell," Mark said when Clara had finished. He looked at Matthew. "When the time comes, if you want out of all this, one way or another I'll buy you out."

"I'll keep that in mind," Matthew replied, fighting the ever-present anger that thoughts of his father created. "That's all I had to discuss this evening." He walked over to the bar and poured himself a jigger of brandy, signaling the end of his participation. Within moments the others began to visit with each other.

"Got another one of those?" Lilly asked, coming to stand next to him.

"Certainly." He poured her a shot of brandy and handed it to her, trying not to notice the sweetly feminine floral scent of her that reached out to surround him.

"Could I speak to you alone after everyone has left?" she asked, her gaze lingering on his face. "I have something I need to discuss with you."

"All right," he agreed, although he had no idea what she needed to talk about with him.

She nodded, sipped her brandy, then walked back to where Clara was seated and crouched down next to the old woman to talk.

Matthew watched her for a long moment, watching the animation of her features as she spoke to Clara. He'd intentionally made himself scarce that afternoon, feeling as if he needed some distance from her.

He'd worked in one of the pastures, fixing fencing and expending enormous energy in an effort to still all the emotions that rolled around inside him.

For some reason, since Lilly's arrival, Matthew had been more on edge, more at odds than he could remember. Something about her appearance here had sparked a cataclysm of emotion that he had yet to be able to sort out.

He turned his attention to his family. Things were changing. Things had changed. The death of their father and the terms of the will he'd left behind had somehow transformed his siblings into different people than they had been.

Mark, who had always been the silent one, as if trying to be invisible, sat straight in his seat with a new sense of pride and self-identity.

Luke, who'd been precariously close to becoming an alcoholic, was facing life sober and with a new sense of responsibility, thanks to his wife and children.

And then there was Johnna, who Matthew had suspected had always been the strongest of them all. She'd managed to leave the ranch to go to college, then had returned to Inferno to build a law practice. It was only the terms of their father's will that had brought her back to spending time on the ranch.

They had all survived their childhood hell and had become thriving, loving people. It amazed him sometimes, the indomitable will of the human spirit.

What angered him more than anything was the fact that their spirits had managed to survive just fine and he was afraid his had not.

He stood just outside the living room window, staring in at the scene inside. The night air that surrounded him was warm, but couldn't compete with the heat inside him as he drank his fill of the sight of Lilly.

Beautiful. Stunning. She looked as good as she had when she'd been sixteen. Even better. And he knew that if the window was open, he'd be able to smell her—a scent that he'd retained in his memory for years.

His blood heated and surged through him, filling him with strength and purpose. She would be his. He knew it in his heart. He recognized it in his very soul.

This afternoon she had stood so close to him he could have reached out his hand and touched her.

He knew just how her skin would feel. He'd dreamed about touching her a thousand times.

And, in the brief words they'd exchanged that afternoon, he'd seen the spark of something secret and knowing in her eyes.

She knew they belonged together. They didn't have to exchange a word. It was a knowledge both of them retained in their souls.

His gaze narrowed as he watched Matthew Delaney pour Lilly a drink. Something in the way he looked at Lilly as he handed her the glass stirred a feeling of threat. For just a moment he thought he saw desire in Matthew's eyes.

"You can't have her," he whispered, his gaze intent on the tall, handsome cowboy. "She's mine."

As he saw the gathering starting to break up, he scurried away from the window and into the night shadows. Fate had given him a second chance to claim Lilly as his own, and he wasn't about to allow Matthew Delaney to stand in his way.

He got into his pickup and headed for his own place, knowing it would be too dangerous to hang around the ranch anymore that evening.

As he drove, he thought again of that look he'd seen in Matthew's eyes as he'd gazed at Lilly. Matthew Delaney would never get an opportunity to follow through on any desire he might feel for Lilly. He would see to that. He would make sure Matthew was too busy with other things to have time for anything remotely resembling romance.

Chapter 4

Lilly had watched the interplay between the Delaney siblings with interest. Never having experienced the joy of sisters or brothers, she'd always had a romanticized version of what sibling relationships should be...and the Delaneys certainly did not fit her perception.

There had been an edge in the tone of voice they'd used with each other, but none as sharp as the edge in Matthew's when he spoke to his brothers and sister.

But that wasn't what she wanted to discuss with him. She knew that the sibling relationship between the Delaneys was none of her business. She simply thought it was sad that four people who should be bonded together through love, common experiences and blood ties didn't seem to be a cohesive family unit at all.

She stood on the front porch, saying goodbye to everyone as they left. She watched as each couple got into their cars and felt a strange sort of longing.

They would all go home and perhaps make love, or spend the night-time hours lying in one another's arms, rehashing the day's events, offering each other support and love.

The twilight time of day was the time Lilly occasionally regretted her choice to live her life alone. Something about facing the end of the day alone was difficult.

As she leaned against one of the porch railings, the longing deepened. Did they realize how very lucky they were? Did they realize how brave it was to open yourself so entirely to another person and trust that they would never hurt you, never abandon you?

She sighed and looked up at the stars that were starting to appear in the sky. Her loneliness tonight felt deeper than usual.

"You wanted to talk to me?"

Lilly jumped in surprise at the sound of Matthew's deep voice behind her. She turned to see him step out onto the porch to join her. "Yes, I did."

He stood just outside the door, looking as handsome as she'd ever seen him in a pair of black dress slacks and a short-sleeved, crisp white cotton shirt that exposed powerful forearms. His thick, dark hair was neatly combed and he looked more like a business executive than a rancher.

"Why don't you come into the kitchen," he suggested. "I just made a short pot of coffee. We can talk in there over a cup."

"All right," she agreed. She followed him back into the house and into the kitchen. The light above the sink was the only illumination. He didn't turn on the big overhead light, but rather went directly to the coffeemaker.

He poured a cup of the fresh brew, then turned to face her. "I'm afraid I don't know how you take your coffee," he said.

She flashed him a quick smile. "You wouldn't know. I wasn't much of a coffee drinker seventeen years ago. Black is fine."

Once the coffee was poured, they sat side by side at the table and he looked at her expectantly. "Thank you for letting me sit in at the family meeting. It was quite interesting," she began.

One of his dark eyebrows rose. "Interesting? Hardly the term I would use to describe our infrequent gatherings." He took a sip of his coffee. "Now what was it you wanted to discuss with me?"

"I was wondering if you knew the name of a good doctor here in town? I'd like to get a complete checkup for Aunt Clara before I leave here."

"Is she ill?"

"No, nothing like that," she assured him. "She's had a couple of dizzy spells and I'd just feel better if she got a complete physical."

"Johnny Howerton is the local doc. I'll dig up his number and give it to you in the morning." He leaned back in his chair, looking more relaxed than he had all evening.

"Thank you. I appreciate it." She sipped her coffee and studied him above the rim of her cup. "Can I ask you a question?"

"If I tell you no will it make any difference?" He offered her a small smile and for just a moment she saw the ghost of the handsome young man she'd enjoyed on those summer days so long ago.

"Probably not," she replied with a grin. She took another drink of her coffee, then wrapped her hands around the mug and looked at him. "Why do you want to sell your share of this place?"

He scowled and stared down into his own mug. "I told you before, I haven't made any final decisions yet."

"But why would you even think about it? It's so beautiful here, and this place holds your roots, your past. Even when you were young, you talked about this place as if it lived and breathed inside of you, was an integral part of who you are."

He was silent for a moment, then his frown deepened and he sat forward. "What difference does it make to you if I sell out or not?" he asked, a touch of impatience in his voice.

"Certainly it doesn't make a difference to me, I was just curious, that's all." She hesitated a moment, then continued, "And I was curious about why you and your brothers and sister are all so angry with each other?"

"I don't know what you're talking about," he replied curtly. "Nobody is angry with anyone." His mouth said one thing, but his eyes said another.

They were gray, stormy depths that radiated with a turbulence that belied his words.

She wasn't sure how far to push or why it seemed so important that she learn more about this man, his moods and the reason for the darkness in his eyes. She decided to lighten the mood. "So what kind of costume are you going to wear to the Halloween party?"

"I don't intend to attend."

"Why not? It sounds like it's going to be lots of fun. I wish I were going to be here to enjoy it."

The storm clouds in his eyes seemed to lighten. "Why can't you be here for it? You said you took a leave of absence from school for the year. What do you have to return to Dallas for?"

"I don't know," she said, then grinned wryly. "My life."

"And what's that like?" His eyes were now the gray stars of warmth she remembered from the distant past, a warmth tempered with a teasing spark. "Is it as wonderful as you used to talk about it being? Have you obtained all those lofty plans you used to spout on about?"

She laughed. "I was pretty sure about what I intended for myself back then, wasn't I?"

A hint of a smile played at the corner of his lips. "So tell me. What kind of life does Lilliana Winstead lead back in Dallas?"

He was close enough to her that she could not only smell his evocative masculine scent, but she could also feel the body heat radiating from him.

Suddenly it was difficult to think, to focus on the question he'd asked her.

"It's a quiet life," she said, and took another sip of her coffee in an attempt to focus on the conversation instead of on the man himself. "I spend the weekdays at school, counseling students, and often in the evenings I have various meetings to attend. I'm a sponsor for several of the student clubs that meet once a week."

"And on the weekends?"

She shrugged. "Saturday mornings I sleep late, then have lunch at a deli near my apartment building. After lunch if the weather is nice, I go for a walk in a park nearby. Then on Saturday nights I have several friends and we all get together and either go to the theater or play cards or just hang out."

Good heavens, she thought in horror. Spoken aloud, her life sounded positively dismal. He pointed to her nearly empty coffee cup, but she shook her head to indicate she wanted no more.

He got up to pour himself more coffee. "Do you date?" he asked with his back to her.

She waited until he was facing her once again before replying. "Not very often anymore. I did the whole dating frenzy thing in my midtwenties like most single people do."

"But no Mr. Right?" He remained standing near the sink rather than joining her back at the table.

"I'm not sure I was ever really looking for Mr. Right." She got up and carried her cup to the sink, where she quickly rinsed it and placed it in the drainer. "I knew from a fairly early age that I'd probably live my life alone. It just seemed right for me.''

At least it had always seemed right to her until tonight, when she'd watched his married siblings leaving arm in arm, two by two.

She mentally shook herself and realized Matthew was staring at her intently. ''What?'' she asked self-consciously.

Again the whisper of a smile curved just the corners of his lips. ''I remember a certain conversation in a hayloft when you told me that you intended to date only older, sophisticated men who could wine you and dine you in the manner you wanted to become accustomed.''

She laughed, instantly remembering the conversation he was referring to. ''Those were the words of a very immature young woman desperately trying to impress a certain young cowboy.''

''Really?'' He set his mug down on the counter and moved closer to where she stood. ''Why on earth would you have wanted to impress me?''

''Oh, Matthew. Don't be obtuse,'' she scoffed, energized by a sudden acceleration of her pulse rate. She tucked a strand of her hair behind her ear and eyed him again. ''You had to have known that I had a terrible crush on you.''

But he hadn't known. She saw by his surprised expression that he hadn't had a clue. There had been times when she'd trembled from his nearness, when her mouth had grown so dry she couldn't talk and her hands had shaken with the need to touch him.

She smiled and shook her head ruefully. ''And

my biggest fear was that I was being too transparent.''

''Either you weren't being that transparent or I really was dumb,'' he replied dryly. ''And the funny thing is, I kind of had a crush on you, too.''

As silly as it was, his words caused her heart to jump. She leaned with her back against the refrigerator. ''You did?'' She sighed dramatically. ''Just think of all those raging, teenage hormones that went to waste because I wasn't transparent enough and you were too dumb to realize just how much I wanted you to kiss me.''

He braced his hand against the refrigerator door just above her head and leaned so close to her she could see the silvery shards that made his eyes such an interesting shade of gray. ''Even if I had known you wanted me to kiss you, I probably wouldn't have done it,'' he said softly.

''Why not?'' Her heart thrummed with a rapid beat at his nearness. The smell of him intoxicated her, a scent of fresh, clean maleness coupled with the slightly spicy hint of cologne. She felt as if she were seventeen years old again, and positively desperate for a kiss from him.

''Because my father would have killed me.''

For a brief moment their gazes remained locked.

''But your father isn't here anymore.'' The words seeped out of her on a mere whisper and were followed by a moment of explosive silence. She felt rather foolish as she realized her words were practically a dare for him to kiss her now.

She pushed herself off the refrigerator and started

to step away from him, but before she could take a single step, he crashed his mouth onto hers.

During her week-long visits over three long, hot summers, she had dreamed of kissing him, but nothing in those girlish imaginings had prepared her for the power, the hunger and the utter thrill of Matthew's kiss.

His mouth took possession of hers at the same time his body leaned into her, subtly forcing her back against the stainless steel refrigerator door.

There was nothing tentative about the kiss. His tongue swirled, touching hers with a heat that was all consuming as he braced his hands against the refrigerator on either side of her.

His upper body pressed against hers, his broad chest against her breasts, but the contact ended there and she fought the desire to push her hips into his, feel her body against the entire length of his.

There was a taste of wildness in his mouth, of hungry desire that stole her breath away. She gasped against him, using her tongue to battle with his.

Someplace in the back of her mind, Lilly was aware of a feeling of barely suppressed energy rolling from him, barely contained control. And for a moment she wished he would snap, completely lose control and make love to her.

Need rose up inside her, a need that seemed too powerful to fight. She didn't want to fight it, she wanted to fall into it, satisfy her need with him. She raised her arms, wanting to wrap them around him, pull him tight against her.

And in that instant he broke the kiss and stepped

back from her, his expression virtually unreadable. "There, now we've satisfied our curiosity," he said. "Good night, Lilly." Without saying another word or without a backward glance, he left her alone in the kitchen.

Lilly remained leaning back, for the first time noticing the coolness of the stainless steel door at her back. She had a feeling if she attempted to take a single step forward, her legs might crumble beneath her. Weak. She was positively weak with want.

And he'd managed that with just a single kiss. If he had touched her in any other way, she had a feeling she would have simply melted away.

Had he kissed her like that in the hayloft so long ago, she had no question that they would have made love. It would have been impossible for her to tell him no...and she wouldn't have wanted to.

Shoving away from the refrigerator, she shut off the coffeemaker and rinsed out the pot, then left the kitchen. A complicated man, she thought as she climbed the stairs to her bedroom. Matthew Delaney was definitely a complicated man.

"Now we've satisfied our curiosity," he'd said, but he was wrong. She was far from satisfied and more curious than ever.

The kiss had been a mistake. A big mistake.

The next morning as Lilly and Matthew began to work to transfer Aunt Clara's belongings from the main house into the cottage, Matthew found himself playing and replaying that kiss in his mind as he had done through the long hours of a long night.

Her lips had been softer than he'd imagined. He'd been surprised by the heat retained in them, a heat that had suffused his entire body as he'd kissed her, a heat that had been as threatening as it had been captivating.

He'd wanted to pull her away from the refrigerator, pull her tight against him so he could feel every inch of her body against every inch of his own.

She now walked just ahead of him, one of Clara's boxes in her arms. He tried not to notice the hypnotic sway of her slender hips, the sinful stretch of her legs and the length of dark, silky hair that swung in rhythm with each one of her steps.

The heat of the kiss had been threatening, because the moment he'd tasted that heat, he'd wanted more. He'd wanted to tangle his fingers in the rich spill of her hair. He'd wanted to rip her clothes off and bury himself in her. And that was not only a threat, it was a clear danger to them both.

He juggled the boxes in his arms and focused his attention away from her. They had been working for the past hour to get Clara settled in and only had her rocking chair left to carry from the main house to her new place.

"Whew!" Lilly exclaimed as she dropped the box she'd been carrying onto the sofa. "It's a good thing Aunt Clara decided to make this move after she had that estate sale."

Matthew set the boxes he'd been carrying down on the floor and tried not to notice how the blue tank top she wore emphasized the brilliant, matching color of her eyes.

"She'll have everything she needs here," he replied. "And what she doesn't have that she thinks she needs, we'll get." She nodded and sent him one of her warm smiles that stirred something rich, yet painful in the very pit of his stomach.

He looked away from her and swiped his hand through his hair. "We'd better get that rocking chair in here because I have other things to do around here besides this."

He sensed her gaze on him and knew he had probably surprised her by the sharpness of his tone. Good. Better she learn that he was a miserable son-of-a-gun and kept her distance from him. That would certainly be best for both of them.

"Fine, let's go get the chair. Then we're finished here," she said.

"You know, I could get somebody else to help me carry this," Matthew said when they'd returned to the main house and were about to pick up the rocking chair. "It's solid and really heavy."

"Don't be silly," she scoffed. She tucked a strand of her long, dark shiny hair behind her ear in a gesture he was finding more and more familiar.

She'd done it often when she'd been young. When in deep thought or slightly nervous or troubled, her fingers moved to tuck her hair. "I'm here now and I can help," she continued. "Between the two of us we should be able to get it with no problem."

Matthew directed her to grab the top of the platform rocker, and he picked up the bottom, where the bulk of the weight was, and together they maneuvered it out the front door.

"Did you know this rocker used to belong to your grandmother?" she asked. She didn't wait for his reply, but continued. "This chair is Aunt Clara's most prized possession. It's the only thing she has from her mother."

"At least she has something," he replied.

Lilly's eyes were soft and achingly blue as she gazed at him. "You don't have anything from your mother?" she asked.

A tight band encircled Matthew's chest. He rarely thought about his mother, Leah, who had died giving birth to Johnna.

Matthew had been five at the time of her death, old enough to have some memories of the beautiful, dark-haired woman. He still remembered the scent of her, a whisper of lilac. And he still remembered how she looked with her eye swollen nearly shut or her lip cut and bloody.

Aware of Lilly's curious gaze on him, he frowned. "No, I don't have anything from her. The day after her funeral, my father packed up everything that had belonged to her and had it hauled away."

They reached the cottage and maneuvered the rocker through the door and set it on the floor. Again she tucked an errant strand of hair behind her ear and gazed at him. "Your father must have been grieving horribly," she said.

It irritated him, how she automatically assumed

his father's motives for getting rid of Leah's things had been born of something good and sterling.

''No. He didn't do it out of grief. He did it out of rage. He was angry at her for dying and leaving him with four brats to raise.'' His words were short and sharp as he fought the building of anger inside him.

''You don't really believe that?'' Her voice held surprise.

''I not only believe it, I know it's true.'' He walked over to the window of the tiny cottage and peered out, his mind suddenly filled with memories of that horrible day. ''I still remember it as if it were yesterday.''

He was vaguely aware of the warmth of her hand on his back and knew she had moved to stand just behind him. He could smell her fragrance wafting in the air. ''Tell me,'' she said softly.

Suddenly he wanted to tell. He felt if he didn't tell he might explode. ''It was one of the worst days of my life,'' he began. He drew a deep breath, going back in time...back to one of the darkest days of his life. ''I can remember Johnna in the crib in the master bedroom. She was so tiny and she was crying so hard and her face was so red I was afraid she was going to die.''

He grabbed hold of the window frame, as if to stabilize himself in the here and now so as not to be lost in the pain of the past. ''My father was raging, tearing mom's clothes out of the closet, shoving things into boxes and cursing her. God, how he was cursing her.''

''What were you doing while all this was going on?'' Her voice held a soft appeal that somehow momentarily eased the pain of the memory.

He drew another deep breath. ''Luke and Mark and I were sitting on the floor at the foot of the bed. That's where father had told us to sit, and we always did as we were told.''

Lilly said nothing, but her hand reached down and grabbed his, squeezing tightly as if by touch alone she could vanquish his memory.

Matthew closed his eyes. ''He got rid of everything that day. Her clothes, her shoes, even her hairbrush. Everything. It was as if he wanted her never to have existed, never to exist at all for us, in memory or thought.''

The band around his chest tightened, bringing with it the rich boldness of the anger that was so much a part of him...the part of himself that frightened him.

He felt that anger building and knew he should tell Lilly to leave him alone...to get away from him. He wanted to tell her that his anger was dangerous...that he was dangerous.

She released his hand and moved to stand between him and the window, forcing him to look at her face, gaze into the soft blue depths of her eyes. ''I'm so sorry, Matthew, that you had to live through that.''

She placed a hand on the side of his face. In the sweet blue waters of her eyes the raging fires of his anger were doused, and he was left with only a deep regret that he'd shared this piece of himself with her, a piece he'd never shared with another person on earth.

"No, I'm sorry," he replied. "I certainly didn't mean to get into all this." He stepped away from her, wanting her touch too much, needing her too much.

"Trust me, Matthew, I know how difficult it is to lose parents when you're young." For just a moment there was a haunted look in her eyes, then she shrugged and smiled. "But we survive, don't we?"

"Survive?" He shoved his hands in his pockets. "I suppose that's what I did."

She looked at him with a directness he found uncomfortable. "And I know the wounds that can be left behind when you lose a parent very young," she said. "But the best thing to do is to talk about it, lance those wounds and let the poison inside go."

"Don't counsel me, Lilly," he warned softly. "Save that for your students at school. Trust me, some scabs are better left alone."

Before she could reply Luke appeared at the door of the cottage. "Matthew, we've got a problem in the guest cottages."

"What kind of a problem?" If nothing else, Matthew was grateful for the interruption in his conversation with Lilly, a conversation that had become much too serious, much too personal.

Luke frowned. "I can't quite explain it. You've got to come and see it."

Together the three of them, Luke, Matthew and Lilly, left the cottage and walked to the group of guest buildings. Luke led them to the first cottage and threw open the door, then stepped back to allow Matthew and Lilly entry.

Matthew stepped in and stared in stunned disbelief.

Lilly gasped in shock.

Spray-paint marred the walls, obscenities and strange symbols scrawled in crimson red. Not a single wall had been left untouched. The artist had apparently exhausted his vocabulary of dirty words.

"Oh, my God," Lilly breathed aloud. "Who would do such a thing?"

"They're all the same," Luke said. "Every cottage has been spray painted. I've already called Sheriff Broder. He should be here anytime."

Matthew nodded and rubbed his forehead wearily. Who would have done such a thing? And why? Unable to stand seeing the chaos of destruction, he stepped back out on the porch. Luke and Lilly followed him, silent and watchful.

"It's going to take nothing short of a miracle to get these cabins ready in three weeks for guests," he said. "I'll have to hire more men or work the ones we have overtime."

"I can paint," Lilly said.

"That isn't necessary," Matthew replied curtly.

"Sure it is," Luke protested. "I can paint and so can Lilly and Abby and Mark. If we all pull together we can get the work done before the guests start arriving."

Matthew said nothing. If the Delaney heirs all pulled together, it would be nothing short of a miracle. And Matthew had given up on miracles years ago.

Chapter 5

It was just after dusk when Lilly joined Matthew on the front porch. He hadn't joined her and Aunt Clara for supper and had spent the afternoon in town buying the paint they would need to redo the walls in the guest cottages.

She sank down in the chair next to his. "You didn't eat," she said.

"I wasn't hungry. Did you get Clara all settled in and unpacked?"

"Yes." Lilly had spent the afternoon, while he'd been in town, helping Aunt Clara unpack her boxes and set out the personal items that would make the cottage feel like home.

"I also called this afternoon and made an appointment with the doctor for her for next week."

Matthew nodded. "Johnny is a good doctor. If there's anything to worry about, he'll tell you."

"I was thinking, with Aunt Clara settled in now she'll probably fix her own meals in the cottage, so that leaves you and me on our own here. Why don't I take over cooking duty," she said.

He shrugged. "Sounds fine to me." He didn't look at her, but continued staring out across the land.

She gazed at him, noting the sharp lines and angles of his face, the determined square chin and straight nose. Something was different about him tonight. In every moment of the time she'd been here, she'd felt a pulsating energy emanating from him. Tonight it was gone.

He looked tired. And beaten. And it bothered her more than she cared to admit. "We'll get the cottages ready in time, Matthew," she said softly.

He sighed and leaned forward in his chair, still not looking at her. "Yeah, I know."

"You heard what Sheriff Broder said, it was probably kids indulging in early Halloween mischief."

"Yeah, I heard what he said." He leaned back once again and turned his head to look at her. "You've asked me a couple of times why I want to sell my share of this place, why I want to leave. It's because there are times I think this place is cursed."

"Cursed?" She eyed him in surprise.

He looked away from her once again and emitted a small, dry laugh. "Ah, don't pay any attention to me. I'm overtired and overreacting to what is, at most, a time-consuming nuisance."

She had a feeling it was much more than that. Matthew didn't seem to be the type of man to overreact to anything. But she also felt him closing off from her, saw the dark shutters appearing in his eyes and knew whatever he was feeling or thinking wasn't going to be shared.

Directing her attention to the landscape, cast in shadows as night fell, she thought of the young man named Danny.

Danny James had been an A student, a nice-looking kid with a sweet smile and dark shutters in his eyes.

Occasionally those shutters would open and in his eyes she'd seen the same kinds of deep shadows that she saw in Matthew's.

Danny James had been a young boy a month away from high school graduation. Danny James had been—she shoved away the thought, knowing to dwell on it would only hurt.

Suddenly she wanted to see Matthew smile, one of those beautiful smiles he used to give her when they were young and life had seemed so much less complicated.

"I've been thinking about what kind of costume you should wear to the Halloween party," she said.

He turned and looked at her again, his eyes glittering like some nocturnal animal in the encroaching darkness. "I told you I wasn't going to the party."

"But if you were going, I think you should go as a wolf...a lone wolf."

"Is that the way you see me?" he asked.

"Isn't that the way you see yourself?" she countered.

He emitted a dry chuckle. "Do you do that on purpose?"

She frowned. "Do what?"

"Make everything some sort of deep, psychological thing."

"I don't do that," she protested.

"Yes, you do, and you did it years ago, too." He now showed more animation than he had all evening. His teeth flashed white as he grinned at her. "You used to ruminate for hours on what made people do what they did."

"I must have been a horrid bore."

"Not at all," he replied, his voice holding a hint of warmth. "You were so passionate about it, trying to make rhyme and find reason for the things people did. I wasn't really surprised when I heard that you'd become a counselor. The only thing that surprised me was that you were working with kids instead of adults."

She shrugged. "I guess I felt as if I had a better chance of saving kids than adults." Again a vision of Danny appeared in her mind, and she consciously shoved it away before it could lay claim to her heart and ache inside her. "So what do you think of my idea?" she asked in an attempt to change the subject.

"What idea?"

"The wolf costume for the Halloween party."

"I told you I'm not planning on attending the party," he replied.

"Well, if you don't go to parties, then what do you do for fun, Matthew?"

"Fun?" He repeated the word as if it were alien to his vocabulary. "I don't have time for fun," he scoffed.

"Everyone needs to make time for fun," she countered. "Come on, Matthew. Agree to attend the party. I'm sure it would mean so much to everyone."

"All right," he relented with a touch of irritation. "I had forgotten how persistent you could be when you got an idea in your head."

"It's what got you into the creek that first day we went wading," she replied with a laugh. "It took a full day of nagging to get you into that water."

"That was fun," he said softly.

"Then we'll do it again...as soon as we get the cottages painted," she said. "Deal?"

He held her gaze intently for a long moment, then he nodded. "Okay, deal." Abruptly he stood. "And now, if you'll excuse me, I'm going to call it a night. I've got a lot of work ahead of me in the next couple of days."

She was disappointed that he was retreating. She would have enjoyed sitting out here in the pleasant evening and talking more, trying to learn more about him as a man. But it seemed for every little piece of information he gave her about himself, he retreated further into a shell of isolation.

It was becoming a habit, this running away that he did from her. It was as if he was afraid she might see too deeply into him.

"And maybe you're reading far too much into

it,'' she mumbled to herself. It was possible the man just didn't find her company particularly enjoyable.

Deciding she might as well go to bed too, she went upstairs to her room. As she undressed, she thought of that kiss they'd shared the night before and had to admit to herself that she wanted to repeat the experience. In fact, she wanted to make love with Matthew Delaney.

She was thirty-five years old, certainly no blushing virgin. She had no illusions about commitment or happily-ever-after and would expect no promises of such from Matthew.

What she did want was to see him lose control, feel the moment when his control snapped and the seething energy she always felt in him exploded. She had a feeling making love to Matthew would be an intense, unforgettable experience.

Clad in her cotton nightgown, she walked over to the window and cracked it open, allowing in the night air. She thought of what Aunt Clara had said, about her staying here and getting a job in Inferno.

There had been times in the darkest hours of the night when she wondered if she even could return to her job at the school in Dallas. Or would she remain too haunted by the thought of a promising young man she had been unable to help?

And why was it that whenever she thought of Danny, her thoughts invariably turned to Matthew? Turning away from the window, she shut off the overhead light and got into bed. Within minutes she was asleep.

She awakened the next morning just after dawn.

She showered quickly and dressed, then went downstairs to the kitchen. Apparently Matthew was already up and out. The coffee had been made but there was no sign of him.

She drank a quick cup of coffee, then left the house and walked to the guest cottages. She found Matthew there, already at work painting with a roller.

For a moment she simply stood in the doorway and watched him work, enjoying the play of his muscles across his broad back as he rolled the paint along the wall.

"If you give me a paintbrush, I'm a good trim man," she said.

He jumped and turned to face her. "You're up early," he said.

She grinned. "I could say the same about you."

"I wanted to get a head start," he replied.

"Then give me a brush. Two painters are definitely a better start than one."

He set his roller down and got her a paintbrush. "Knock yourself out," he said, then turned back to his work.

For a few minutes they painted in silence. "We could speculate on what kind of person would do something like this," she finally said to break the silence.

He turned and cast her a painful glance. "Must we?"

She laughed. "Okay, then we can talk about what your favorite foods are so I'll know what to cook each evening."

"Are you a good cook?" he asked curiously.

"I've never killed anyone with my cooking," she replied.

He laughed. "That's certainly a good recommendation if ever I heard one."

As easily as that they fell into a conversation much like the ones they had once enjoyed. They argued about politics, talked of places they'd visited, sights they had seen.

She told him about the summers she'd spent working at a youth camp, where she'd not only counseled children, but had also painted, cut grass, and done a variety of other odd jobs.

He talked to her about his father's decision to turn the ranch into a dude ranch and the work that had been involved in transforming the place from a private home to a working resort.

And with each word that was exchanged, Lilly sensed a new relaxation in Matthew. His eyes sparkled and there were no tension lines marring his handsome face.

The only time she was conscious of a burst of tension radiating from him was when they stood too close together or when their shoulders brushed while they worked. It was then she felt the tension, saw the flare of something in his eyes, and knew he wasn't as unaffected by her nearness as he'd like to pretend he was.

This knowledge affected her, building in her a corresponding tension that was both irritating yet bewitching. Again she found herself wondering what it would be like to make love with him, to feel those powerful arms of his wrapped tightly around her, to lose herself in the darkness of his eyes and the absolute intensity of the act.

It was about ten o'clock when Johnna and Jerrod arrived, ready for paint duty and soon after that Mark and Luke's wife, Abby showed up.

"I told April to stay at home," Mark said. "With her being pregnant, I didn't think the paint fumes would be good for her. And Luke said to tell you he'll be here later, he had some things to take care of this morning."

Matthew nodded, lines of tension back in his forehead. "Then let's get to work," he said.

Within minutes everyone had a paintbrush or a roller, and despite the circumstances that had brought them all together, a party atmosphere appeared.

At noon Aunt Clara arrived, bringing with her a tray of sandwiches and a pitcher of lemonade. They took a quick break to eat, then got back to work.

As Lilly painted, she once again found herself watching the byplay between the Delaney siblings and wondering why Matthew seemed so isolated from the others. He was a lone wolf in what should have been a pack.

It was nearing noon when Luke appeared at the door of the cottage they were all now painting. "Matthew?" Luke's face was set in grim lines. "We have another problem," he said.

"What now?" Matthew asked.

"I was just out at the old barn. The supplies that

were delivered yesterday morning? Half of them are gone now.''

''Gone? What do you mean, gone?'' Johnna asked.

Luke shrugged. ''Disappeared. Vanished. Stolen. I don't know what happened to them, but they're gone.''

Matthew raked a hand through his hair. ''What in the hell is going on around here?'' he asked nobody in particular.

And nobody had an answer for him.

Matthew sat on the baled hay in the hayloft of the old barn, staring out the opened loft door toward the main house and outbuildings of the ranch in the distance.

He'd spent most of the afternoon in town at the lumber yard, trying to figure out exactly what had been stolen and what needed to be reordered. He'd then gone to Sheriff Broder's office and had filed another report.

He lay back on an old blanket on top of the hay and stared up at the rafters. He might have been able to agree with Broder and write off the spray-painted cottages as preHalloween mischief, but the robbery of the materials made him rethink everything.

He just couldn't believe it had been kids who had loaded up that material and hauled it off. Matthew had a feeling it was something much more sinister than mischief. But what? Who was responsible? And what did they hope to accomplish?

He drew a deep breath, his head filling with a

vision of Lilly. He'd enjoyed her company that morning while the two of them had painted. She'd been a charming and entertaining companion on those summer days so long ago, and she hadn't lost those qualities in the intervening years.

Again he found himself thinking of the kiss they had shared and felt a stir of hunger awaken inside him. He had wanted Lilly when he'd been sixteen, when he'd been seventeen and the last time he'd seen her, when they'd been eighteen. And it surprised and vaguely irritated him that he still wanted her.

Consciously he shoved aside thoughts of her and instead thought of his family.

As always, when all of them were together, whether working or socializing, Matthew felt a curious aloneness.

He'd always prided himself on being a solitary man who needed nobody, but watching his siblings interact so easily with each other that afternoon had bothered him.

For just a moment he'd wanted to laugh with them, be able to forget the past and reach out to each of them, but he couldn't...and he wasn't sure why.

The sound of horse hooves pounding the ground drew him up from his prone position and he looked out the loft door to see Lilly approaching on horseback.

She rode the way she did everything else—wholeheartedly. It was one of the qualities about her that had always drawn him. She seemed to embrace all of life, without fear and without reservation.

He wasn't sure if he was glad to see her or irritated that she had managed to hunt him down. His nerves were pulled taut enough as it was and he wasn't sure if her presence would make things worse or better.

He watched as she dismounted and tied her horse next to his, then heard her open the door below. "Matthew?" Her voice carried easily in the otherwise stillness of the barn.

He thought of keeping silent, unsure if he wanted her company or not. "I'm up here," he called out after a moment of hesitation.

A moment later her head popped up in the loft near where he was sprawled. "You missed supper," she said. Her hair was tousled, and the exertion of the ride had whipped a pleasing color into her cheeks.

"What did I miss?"

She climbed up into the loft the rest of the way and sank down beside him on the blanket. "Tuna surprise. The surprise is that it tastes like tuna at all."

He knew she was trying to make him smile, but he simply couldn't work up the energy for even that simple gesture. He stared out the loft door, aware of her gaze on him.

"Matthew? Are you all right?"

He opened his mouth to tell her that of course he was all right, that he'd simply come here to be alone and avoid talking to anyone. "I don't know," he surprised himself by replying.

Again he focused his gaze out to the distance. "I've just been sitting up here trying to figure out what's going on."

"Did you come up with any answers?"

He shook his head. "Nothing that makes any kind of sense."

She stretched out on her side next to him, her elbow propping her up. "Did they steal a lot from here?"

"Enough." Once again he lay on his back and stared at the roof beams, intensely aware of her so close to him. Where before the only scent in the air had been the odor of hay and a lingering hint of horseflesh, now the air was redolent with the scent of her.

Her nearness had bothered him all morning as they had painted together. Clad in a coral-colored tank top that exposed the faintest hint of the top of her breasts, and in another pair of those shorts that made her legs appear impossibly long, she had been a source of temptation. And the temptation certainly hadn't diminished.

With the scent of her and the hay around him, if he closed his eyes he could almost imagine them back in time. They had spent a lot of hours in this hayloft trying to solve world problems. Even in the midst of one of their serious conversations, Matthew had never lost sight of her attractiveness.

"Do you have any idea who might be responsible?" Her soft voice intruded on his thoughts.

He turned to his side and propped himself on his elbow, so they were face-to-face and only mere inches apart. "I don't have a clue," he replied.

She frowned, her eyes slightly deeper in hue than usual. "What about somebody from the development company that wants to buy this place?"

"Why would they want to make this kind of trouble for us?" he asked, fighting the impulse to reach out and touch a strand of her dark, shiny hair. He knew it would be wonderfully silky.

"I don't know. Maybe they want to make problems, then renegotiate a lower price."

"Maybe," he said, although he didn't believe it. "Or, maybe Jacob Tilley is paying back the Delaneys for his father being in prison."

Her eyes widened. "You really think so?"

He rolled onto his back again, finding it much easier to concentrate on the conversation if he wasn't looking at her. "Who knows. Sometimes I just get the feeling that this place is cursed."

"You mentioned that last night." She placed a hand on his forearm. "Cursed by whom? By what?"

Her hand was warm...too warm, and he wanted to shake it off him. How could he tell her that he felt as if this land, this ranch was cursed by the spirit of a miserable man? How could he tell her that the specter of his father seemed to be in every room, in every corner, and there would never be any happiness found here because of his ghostly presence.

"Forget it," he said. He sat up and faced the loft door, his back to her. He drew a deep breath, wondering why at this moment all his emotions seemed so close, too close, to the surface?

"Matthew, talk to me. Tell me what you're thinking...what you're feeling." She was silent for a moment, then continued. "You seem so alone."

"I like being alone."

"Well, right now you aren't alone." She crawled over to sit next to him, and for several long minutes they simply sat and stared out into the distance. The sun was riding low in the sky, sending out a splash of farewell colors in pinks and oranges.

"It's beautiful from up here." She finally broke the silence.

"Yes, it is," he replied grudgingly. He couldn't dispute the beauty of the land...their land...his father's land.

"Don't you want to have a son or daughter to pass all this onto?" she asked, then didn't wait for his reply. "That's the only thing I regret about never marrying, the fact that I'll never have children."

"You could have a child without marriage. Women do it all the time."

She shook her head, her hair swaying around her shoulders with the movement. "That's never been an option for me. I guess I'm more conservative than I thought."

He frowned thoughtfully and cast his gaze once again out the loft door. "I should have left this place a long time ago, made my own way somewhere else."

"Why didn't you?"

"Because I had to stay. I had to protect them."

The words fell from his mouth unbidden and were met with a long moment of silence.

"Protect them? You mean your sister and brothers?" Again she placed a hand on his arm. "Protect them from what?"

He hesitated before replying, wondering if he would later regret this conversation, yet suddenly unable to stop himself from having it. "From my father, who was the meanest bastard on the planet."

He turned and looked at her and fought the anger that always surged inside him at thoughts of Adam Delaney. "I had to stick around and make sure things ran smoothly, do the right thing to keep him happy and hope to God when he did have one of his explosions he didn't manage to kill me or one of them."

Her eyes widened, and her hand gently squeezed his forearm. "Your father was abusive?"

"My father was a sick son-of-a-bitch who took pleasure in beating and tormenting his children." Matthew heard the venom in his voice and drew another deep breath to steady himself. "He was physically and mentally abusive every day of our lives."

"Oh, Matthew."

He turned to look at her, and his breath was nearly stolen away by the sweet empathy of her expression, the gentleness and compassion in her eyes. He shrugged and emitted a small laugh of embarrassment. "It doesn't matter anymore. It's all in the past, anyway."

She placed a hand on the side of his face, her

fingers stroking softly down his cheek. "I'm so sorry, Matthew. I had no idea."

He shrugged, a bitter smile on his face. "How could you know? The old man was always on his best behavior while you were here."

He pulled her hand from his face, but instead of releasing it, held it in his own and stared down at it. She had pretty hands, slender and long-fingered, and her nails were painted a pretty pearlized pink. Her hand was warm, and he was surprised to feel some of his anger dissipate as he held it.

"Those weeks that you were here visiting were the very best weeks of my life," he said softly. "I knew that during the time you were here my father wouldn't beat me or any of the other kids. For that week I could pretend that we were a normal family and we had a normal father."

Her fingers curled around his and he felt the stir of a tension that had nothing to do with thoughts of his father. He released her hand and stood and moved to the loft door, needing to distance himself from her nearness, from her touch. If he didn't get some distance, he wasn't sure what he might do.

"But there was always a consequence to that week of no beatings," he continued. He rubbed the center of his forehead with two fingers as he thought of those days so long ago. "The day that you and Clara left I'd get the beating of my life."

"For what?" she asked as she stood up and moved behind him.

He turned back and looked at her with a wry, humorless smile. "For whatever. I got hit for being nice to you and for not being nice enough. I got slapped for the way I'd looked at you over the dinner table, for *not* looking at you while we were eating dinner.''

He shrugged and once again focused his attention back to the distance. "I think he knew I liked you, and he wanted to taint that, ruin it. He knew I had fun with you, enjoyed your company, and so he always made sure I paid.''

She took his hand and pulled him around to face her. Her eyes shone with a shimmering light that made his chest ache. "He's not here to make you pay anymore,'' she said softly, then she leaned forward and placed her lips on his.

With his emotions so close to the surface, he had no defenses against the onslaught of heat and the taste of desire that was ripe in her mouth.

It was what he'd feared...and what he'd wanted.

A groan of pleasure escaped him as he wrapped his arms around her and pulled her tightly against him, returning her kiss with a savage hunger that felt as if it had burned in him for her for years.

When he finally broke the kiss, she stepped back from him and stretched out on the bed of hay. "Make love to me, Matthew.'' Her voice was an urgent whisper of need. "Make love to me now like you wanted to then. There's nobody to punish us, and I promise there won't be any consequences.''

As if to break the inertia that held him in place, she reached down and grabbed the bottom of her tank top and pulled it off over her head, exposing to him the nude-colored bra that did little to hide her breasts.

In an instant he knew he was going to make love to her, he knew it would be a mistake, knew that even though his father wasn't around to punish him, eventually he would punish himself.

But at that moment all the reasons why they shouldn't do this were distant cries that echoed faintly, overridden by the white-hot streak of desire that seared through him.

With a fevered groan, he sank down on the hay and took her back into his arms.

Chapter 6

As Matthew drew her against him on the soft bed of hay, Lilly felt as if this moment in time had been destined long ago. It was as if all those hours they had spent talking together, laughing together, so long ago had been a kind of foreplay that now would come to fruition.

His confession about his father had stunned her. She'd had no idea what the Delaney children had suffered at the hands of their father. Matthew's pain, when he'd told her about the past, had filled the loft and seeped into her heart to the point where all she wanted to do was somehow erase that pain.

But all thoughts of his father and abuse disappeared from her head as Matthew claimed her lips in a kiss of intense hunger and sweet mastery. It was impossible, as his hands ran up the length of her back and his lips plied hers with flames, to think of anything but making love to him.

Her heart beat a quicksilver rhythm as their kiss deepened. She placed her hands on either side of his face, loving the feel of the faint scrub of whiskers there, the strength of his jawline just beneath the emerging beard.

He broke the kiss only long enough to sit up and pull his T-shirt over his head, then captured her mouth again as her hands raked across the broad width of his bare back and her legs twined with his.

Endless moments were spent in kissing, their tongues touching, seeking, then retreating and beginning anew. There was a wildness in his kiss that intoxicated her and with the press of their bodies so close, she could feel his hardness against her. It filled her with a need so yawning and rich, a need such as she'd never known before.

"Lilliana," he finally uttered against her hair, into her ear as his fingers worked the clasp of her bra.

"Matthew," she replied, loving the sound of her name on his lips, the feel of his name on hers. She moaned as her bra fell away and his hands cupped her breasts.

His thumbs raked across her nipples, and they responded, rising to pebble hardness and aching with sweet sensation. She pulled his head down, wanting to feel his tongue on them.

He complied, using the tip of his tongue to tease and torment, sending her higher up the spiral of desire. As his mouth pleasured her breasts, his fingers danced across her stomach at the waistband of her shorts.

His hands were hot, fevered, and it was a fever she relished, a fever that burned inside her, as well. As his hands worked the button snap of her shorts, her fingers did the same to his jeans.

Impatience made her fingers clumsy. She wanted to feel his nakedness against hers. She wanted no barriers between them. As if he felt the same way, he gently shoved her hands aside and stood.

With his gray eyes burning into hers, he unsnapped his jeans and slid them off. For a moment she had a glimpse of him clad only in a pair of navy briefs, and his beauty stunned her. Then the briefs were gone and he knelt down and grabbed the waist of her shorts.

In slow, deliberate movements, he pulled her shorts off and threw them aside, leaving her only in a pair of wispy silk panties.

She shivered, instinctively knowing she was about to be loved more thoroughly, more passionately than she'd ever been loved in her life. She saw it in the flames of his eyes, felt the crackle of electric heat that sizzled in the air.

"You are so beautiful." The words eased out of him as if from beneath an enormous pressure.

She wanted to tell him that he was beautiful, too, that his broad shoulders stirred her, his muscled abdomen awed her, and his arousal stole her breath away. But she got no opportunity to say anything, for once again he was against her and his mouth took utter possession of hers.

As he kissed her, his hands worked her panties down and she aided his efforts, arching her hips up to meet his intimate touch.

She felt as if she'd been ready for that touch for years, and it shattered her. As he stroked her she cried out and rode a crest of pleasure so intense it melted her from the inside out.

For a long moment she remained motionless, gasping from the sheer power of her release, then she reached a hand down and encircled him.

He gasped and froze, not moving a muscle. She thought she could hear his heartbeat pounding in the otherwise silent loft. But she wasn't sure if it was his or her own.

She looked into his eyes as she stroked the length of him, saw the haze of desire that darkened his beautiful eyes, felt the stiffening of his body at the sensual assault.

"That's dangerous," he said, his voice filled with simmering tension.

"Yes," she replied and stroked him again, this time with her fingers tightened slightly around him. She sensed that his control was fragile, and she wanted that control to break. She wanted him beyond control, wild with want.

She wanted all those seething emotions she'd felt in him since she'd arrived here to break free and consume him...consume her.

And as she stroked him a third time, that control snapped. With a muffled curse, he removed her hand from him and moved between her legs and entered her.

He didn't ease in, but buried himself inside her, and they both froze, overwhelmed by the sensations of their joining.

Lilly was enflamed, lost to any other conscious thought as he filled her up. His mouth again sought hers, and as he kissed her, tears sprang to her eyes...tears of pleasure so intense she thought she might die.

He moved against her, slowly at first, easing in and out in an age-old rhythm that set Lilly's nerve endings on fire. As he increased the pace, she matched him thrust for thrust as she once again began to climb toward the pinnacle of desire.

Faster and faster, in frenzied need, they clung to one another as outside the twilight deepened and cast dancing shadows through the loft.

Sensation whirled in her, taking her up...up...up to peaks never before realized, and then she was there, falling over the edge as he stiffened and cried out her name in sweet release.

Minutes passed and they remained unmoving, their bodies still locked together. Their breathing slowed...calmed, and Lilly's heartbeat resumed a more normal pace.

Still, she didn't move from his embrace. She wanted to remain locked in his arms forever. She wanted to lie in his arms through the night and watch the sunrise from his embrace.

"We should have done this years ago," she said, finally breaking the silence.

He rolled to the side of her and wrapped a strand of her hair around his finger. "No, we shouldn't have. We were too young to handle it then. It would have complicated things.''

His features were obscured by the deep shadows that had begun to claim the loft. ''Maybe you're right,'' she agreed. ''Although at the time I thought I was mature enough to handle anything.''

He smiled. ''And that's a sure sign that you were too immature.'' He unwrapped her hair from his finger and instead trailed his hand down the side of her face.

She gazed at him. ''Why didn't you ever tell me about your father?'' she asked softly. Instantly she knew the question was a mistake.

Stress rolled toward her from him, and he sat up abruptly and swiped a hand through his hair. ''Because I knew there was nothing you could do.''

''I could have told Aunt Clara,'' she replied, and also rose to a sitting position.

In one graceful movement, he stood and grabbed his jeans. ''It's getting dark. You need to get back to the house.''

She reached out and picked up her bra, sorry she'd broken the mood, sorry she'd brought up the topic of his father once again. ''What about you? Aren't you coming back to the house?''

''I'll go back later.'' He pulled on his jeans.

''I'll wait for you.''

''No,'' he replied sharply. He grabbed her shorts and tossed them to her. ''This was all a mistake, Lilly. It would have been a big mistake years ago, and it was a bigger mistake now.''

The shaft of pain that swept through her at his

words surprised her. She didn't want him deriding what they had just shared, not with the scent of him still clinging to her skin, not with the taste of him still in her mouth.

"If it was a mistake, it was an overwhelmingly pleasant one," she said dryly. She quickly stepped into her panties, feeling naked and vulnerable where before she'd felt naked and beautiful.

He shoved his hands in his pockets. "Yeah, it was, but just because it felt good doesn't mean it wasn't a mistake. I don't want or need a woman in my life. I don't want or need anyone in my life."

Lilly wanted to argue with him, to tell him that she'd never seen anyone who needed as much as he did, but she knew now was not the time or the place. He'd completely closed off from her. The shutters in his eyes were firmly in place, obscuring any emotion that might shine there.

"I'll wait downstairs while you finish getting dressed," he said and headed down the ladder to the barn below.

Lilly finished getting dressed and hurried down to where he waited next to their horses. His features were stony and grim, no hint of the softer man who had just made love to her.

It angered her just a little, how quickly he'd been able to shut her out. As he held her horse's bridle, she mounted. "I'm sorry, Matthew, that your father was a mean, hateful bastard," she said. "But that doesn't mean you have to become one. The past is over and done, and you only have control over what you do with your future."

She yelped in surprise as he gave her horse a sharp slap on the rump. The horse shot forward and she grabbed wildly for the reins and slowed the horse's pace.

She'd gone only a short distance when she turned in the saddle and looked back at the barn.

Matthew stood in the shadows of night, staring after her, and never had she seen a man who looked so achingly alone.

"Thanks for meeting with me, Judd," Matthew said to the dark-haired man seated across the table from him in the Inferno café.

Judd Stevens nodded, his green eyes sharp and assessing. "You said on the phone you're having some problems out at the ranch. So what's going on?"

Judd Stevens was an ex-FBI agent who had worked on occasion for Matthew's sister as a private investigator. Matthew knew little about the man other than Johnna liked and trusted him, and that Judd had moved to Inferno several years ago after quitting the FBI.

Quickly Matthew told him about the destruction in the cabins and the lumber and supplies that had been stolen four days previous. "The latest incident took place yesterday," he said. "One of the workers thought an opened bag of feed looked and smelled funny. It was funny all right, somebody had laced it with enough rat poison to kill any horse that might have eaten some of it."

Judd's eyes narrowed and he took a sip of his

coffee. "Nasty stuff," he finally said. "So what do you want from me?"

"I'm not sure," Matthew admitted. "I don't even know if the person responsible for all this is working at the ranch or not."

"Have you had a beef with anyone? Know any reason why somebody would want to cause you grief?" Judd asked.

Matthew frowned. "Walter Tilley went to prison for transporting aliens and killing a social worker from the ranch. He was caught by us right before he was going to kill my brother, Mark, and his wife. Jacob Tilley, Walter's son, just recently came to work for me."

"And you think he might be getting revenge for his father?"

Matthew sighed and leaned back in the seat. "I don't know. He seems genuinely appalled by his father's crimes. He doesn't seem to hold a grudge against us, but he's the only one I can think of who might have a reason to cause us problems."

Frustration surged up inside him, a frustration that had been building for days. "I figured I'd talk to you and see if you had any suggestions. We're going to have guests arriving in two weeks, and I don't want anything going on that might put any of them at risk."

Judd took another sip of his coffee. "The first thing I would recommend you do is talk to a few of the men you trust, see if they've seen anyone acting suspicious, pay them extra to work extra hours to keep an eye on things."

Matthew nodded. "I've already done that. I've got a couple of men who have been with me for years."

"Other than that, I'm not sure there's a whole lot you can do. You might want to check the backgrounds of all the people who work for you," Judd suggested. "I'm not sure you'll find any answers, but you might get something that sends up a red flag."

"Can you do that? Check backgrounds?"

Judd nodded. "Sure, if you get me the information. Get me copies of their job applications, and I'll see what I can come up with. You might want to bring me the applications of anyone who has left your employ over the past couple of months also."

"You know you're probably going to find false information on a lot of those applications," Matthew said. "Ranch hands are often transients, working for a few months, then moving on. They aren't always completely honest when it comes to job applications."

Judd smiled. "Then we'll see who is lying and why."

Matthew nodded and looked at his watch. "I've got to get out of here. I dropped my aunt at a doctor's appointment and she should be about finished by now." Matthew finished up his coffee and stood. "I'll get those applications to you in the next day or two."

A moment later Matthew stepped out of the café and headed down the sidewalk toward the doctor's office. With each step he took, he steeled himself for seeing Lilly once again.

He'd seen little of her over the course of the past four days, had consciously kept physical distance between them. He left the house just after dawn and returned after dusk to find a plate of whatever she had cooked for dinner awaiting him.

He had no idea how she had spent her days. He had spent his trying to forget. He wanted to forget the taste of her mouth, so hot and sweet against his. He wanted to forget the silky heat of her skin, her breathy little moans and the exquisite pleasure of making love to her.

Every day he'd worked himself to exhaustion. The family had pulled together and there were only two guest cottages left to repaint. One of them would probably be done by the time they returned to the ranch this afternoon. When they'd left for the doctor's appointment, Abby and Luke had already been painting.

Matthew had stayed away from the guest cottages and let his family take care of them. Instead, he had spent his days out at the old barn where Cal Simmon, the contractor in charge of the renovations, had begun work.

Matthew had offered his services as a laborer. He'd helped carry and tote, hammer and saw. He'd worked hard enough that each night he'd fallen into bed exhausted. And still he thought of Lilly, dreamed of her.

He entered the doctor's office. Nobody sat behind the receptionist's desk, and Lilly was the only person in the waiting room. Clad in a turquoise sundress that did dazzling things to her eyes, she looked up from the magazine she'd been reading and smiled at him.

"Did you get your business taken care of?" she asked as he sat in the chair next to hers.

He nodded, trying not to notice the familiar scent of her, fighting against a visceral response. He knew now that the scent she wore was strongest between her breasts and just beneath each of her ears. "Has anyone said how much longer Clara is going to be?" he asked.

"No, but it shouldn't be too much longer."

He stared at the door through which Clara would come, aware of Lilly's gaze lingering on him. This was the first time they'd been alone since making love. He'd gone out of his way the past four days to make sure they didn't have any time alone.

"You've been avoiding me," she said softly.

"I've been busy," he replied, not looking at her.

"No, it's more than that." She closed the magazine and set it on the coffee table in front of them. "You don't have to worry, Matthew. Just because we made love doesn't mean I'm going to somehow turn into a sappy, clinging woman desperate for a relationship with you. I know you don't want to get married, and you know I don't want to, either."

"I don't want to discuss it," he replied stiffly.

"Tough," she shot back.

He turned to look at her then. Her eyes sparked with irritation, and her chin was thrust upward like a pugnacious fighter. "I told you that it was a mistake."

"Fine, it was a mistake, but you don't have to punish me forever."

"I'm not punishing you," he scoffed. "I told you, I've been busy."

"Too busy to share a simple meal with me? You've missed dinner every night this week." She leaned toward him, enveloping him with her scent, enflaming him with her nearness. "What are you afraid of, Matthew? Afraid you might just want to repeat our mistake?"

He was saved from having to reply by Clara and Dr. Johnny Howerton exiting the examining rooms. As they entered, both Lilly and Matthew stood. Matthew offered his hand to the doctor.

"Johnny, good to see you again," he said.

"You, too, Matthew." They shook hands. "Well, she appears to be in pretty good health," he said. "We did everything we could do here in the office, but I've scheduled some additional tests for next week at the hospital."

"What kind of tests?" Lilly asked, a worry wrinkle creasing her forehead.

"I'd like to get an electrocardiogram and an echocardiogram on her. Neither test takes long, but at her age and with the little 'spells' she's told me she's had, I'd like the tests done just to be on the safe side."

"A bunch of nonsense," Clara said a moment later as they left the doctor's office. "I'm perfectly healthy," she exclaimed. "I just get a little dizzy every now and then. I've always been a little dizzy.''

"We're still going to see to it that you get those tests,'' Lilly said as she placed an arm around the old woman's shoulders.

Clara nodded, then looked at Matthew. "Matthew, dear, would you mind stopping at the grocery store before we head back to the ranch? There are a few things I'd like to pick up.''

"You know you're welcome to anything that is at the ranch. We have freezers full of meat and pantries filled with canned goods.''

She nodded. "And I thank you for that, but it's enough that you're allowing me to stay in the cottage rent-free. I insist on buying my own food.'' Pride stiffened her back. "I like to think I'm taking care of myself at least a little bit.''

"Fine, we'll stop by the grocery store,'' he said curtly. What he wanted more than anything was to get back to the ranch and get some much-needed distance from Lilly. In just the brief time he'd spent with her today, renewed desire for her had reawakened with a vengeance.

Within minutes Matthew was parked in front of the grocery store, and Clara disappeared inside. Matthew got out of the car and walked to a bench in front of the store and sat down. A moment later, to his irritation, Lilly joined him there.

"Aunt Clara's pride has taken quite a beating,'' she said, and stretched her tanned, slender legs out before her.

Matthew didn't reply. He focused his gaze toward the street as tension welled up inside him.

"Why don't you call her Aunt Clara?"

"Excuse me?" Despite his reluctance, he turned to look at her. "What are you babbling about?"

His words seemed to do nothing to deter her. "Aunt Clara," she replied. "You always refer to her as just Clara."

"And your point?"

She shrugged. "Just curious." Her gaze lingered on him. "You don't like her very well, do you?"

"Don't be ridiculous. She's an old woman. She's my aunt. Why shouldn't I like her?" he countered.

"I don't know. That's what I'm trying to figure out. You seem cold and distant with her."

"Lilly, not everything is deep and psychological, and I think the biggest problem you have is that you think far too much."

"You're probably right," she agreed easily. "I've always thought too much...especially about the people I care about. But you wouldn't know about that, right?" There was an edge of sarcasm to her tone.

Matthew leaned his head back and drew a deep breath. The woman was absolutely impossible. "Lilly, I don't want to fight with you," he said wearily.

"And I don't want to fight with you," she replied softly. She touched his arm, her eyes beseeching as she gazed at him. "I'm worried about you, Matthew. You seem so angry all the time."

"Hell yes, I'm angry." He stood, unable to sit another minute. "Somebody has spray-painted cottages, stolen property and tried to poison my horses. I'd say I have a right to be angry.''

''Yes, you do,'' she replied and also stood. ''As long as your anger is directed in the right place. What worries me is that I don't think it is.''

Again she placed a hand on his arm and this time he grabbed it and held it away from him. He knew she had no idea that her simplest touch was torture for him, stirred a desire that suffocated him with need.

''You're right, Lilly. I'm an angry man, and the best thing you can do is stay away from me. Stay the hell out of my head and out of my life.'' He released her hand and walked back to the car.

He climbed into the driver's seat, grateful that she hadn't attempted to come after him, but had disappeared into the store.

Chapter 7

"Tell me about your father," Lilly said to Johnna the next day. The two women had been working together for the past hour, finishing up the painting in the last guest cottage.

Johnna looked at her in surprise. "Why on earth would you want to know anything about him?"

Lilly shrugged and scratched the end of her nose with the handle of her paintbrush. "Matthew mentioned that he was difficult."

"That's a surprise. Matthew never talks about Father. And if he told you Father was difficult, then he managed to utter the understatement of the century."

Johnna set her paintbrush down, stretched her arms overhead, then frowned at Lilly. "He was a mean man, Lilly. I can't remember a day of my childhood that I wasn't afraid. We were all afraid all the time. Of course, Matthew probably wasn't as afraid as the rest of us. He was the good son, pouring father his drinks or getting his slippers. I don't remember him getting the beatings the rest of us got.''

''Is that why the three of you seem so close and Matthew seems so separate from you?'' Lilly asked curiously.

Johnna's frown deepened. ''Matthew is separate from us because he chooses to be. He's always been stern and unyielding, but since father died, he's been so...so...''

''Angry?''

Johnna nodded. ''Yes. Exactly. He wasn't so bad before father's death. But now you can see it in his eyes all the time, feel it rolling off him. More and more he reminds me of Father.'' Johnna eyed her in speculation. ''Don't go there, Lilly.''

''Go where?''

''Don't try to get close to Matthew. He'll only hurt you in the end. He doesn't want to let anyone into his life. I think, somehow, of all of us, he's the most scarred.''

Lilly smiled at Johnna reassuringly. ''Don't worry, I'm a big girl and I'm not looking to get into his life. I have a perfectly satisfactory life of my own back in Dallas. I was just curious, that's all.''

''Yeah, well, you know what they say about curiosity...''

Lilly laughed. ''I'm not a cat so I'm not real worried about those kind of consequences.''

Their conversation turned to the Halloween party

April was planning. Although Lilly didn't mention it to Johnna, she'd made the decision not to stick around for the party. Once Aunt Clara had her tests and got the results back, Lilly intended to leave to return to Dallas.

Her mind had been changed the day before, when Matthew had grabbed her arm and told her to stay out of his head and out of his life. She had realized at that moment there was no point in her hanging around here any longer than necessary, that Matthew was as lost a cause as Danny had been.

By noon they had the cottage painted and together they piled the brushes in the sink. "We need to get these clean because I've got to get out of here," Johnna said as she looked at her watch. "I've got to be in court later this afternoon."

"Then go," Lilly said. "I can do the cleanup here."

Johnna hesitated. "Are you sure?"

Lilly shoved her toward the door. "Go on, get out of here."

Johnna flashed her a grin. "Thanks, Lilly."

As Johnna left the cottage, Lilly went back to the sink and began to rinse out the brushes and paint pans. As she worked she thought of what Johnna had said about Matthew.

He'd been the good son, the one who had tried to control the violence in the house by making sure there was nothing to get angry about. But, of course, he couldn't make things right, hadn't been in control of his father's rage.

It must have been horrible, growing up in a house

where you never knew what might set off a violent man, being so afraid all the time. Lilly's heart broke not only for Matthew but also for his brothers and sister. Still, they had managed to get past the old wounds, open themselves up to others. Why couldn't Matthew?

"Whoa! I didn't know you were in here."

Lilly whirled around from the sink to see Eddie entering the cottage. "Hi, Eddie. I'm just cleaning up paintbrushes," she said and shut off the faucet.

He nodded. "The boss man told me to do a final check on everything in the cottages, then lock them up tight." He frowned. "Damn shame what somebody did to all these."

"Yes, it was," she agreed.

"I heard you were from Dallas," he said, and leaned against the small table.

"Yes, I am. You ever been there?" She grabbed a rag and dried off the brushes.

"Years ago. I worked a ranch just outside of Plano. Nice place, not as hot as it is here."

She gathered up the brushes and pans. "So how do you like working here for the Delaneys?" she asked.

"It's all right. When you're a ranch hand one place is about as good as another."

"Well, I'll just leave you to your work," she said, and with a smile, left the cottage.

She put the paint supplies away in a storage bin in the stables, then walked toward the house. What she wanted more than anything at the moment was a hot shower, then some lunch.

The house was silent when she entered, and she assumed Matthew was out in the field working somewhere. She went up to her bedroom, grabbed clean clothes, then went into the bathroom and within minutes stood beneath a hot spray of water.

She knew she was foolish for wanting to help Matthew, especially when he so clearly didn't think he needed and didn't want any help. She suspected that part of her need to do something to ease the shadows in his eyes had to do with the tragedy that had forced her to take a leave from her job.

But what worried her most was the part of her need to see those shadows dissipate that had nothing to do with her professional interest. As a woman she would love to see those beautiful gray eyes of his clear and lit with happiness. She'd love to hear his laughter ringing out frequently, see his body relaxed instead of racked with tension.

She shut off the water in the shower and grabbed a towel. Drying off, she told herself that Matthew Delaney was not her concern and in a week she'd leave here...and him to go back to Dallas.

She would return to her life and forget the boy she had spent those distant summers with, forget the man she'd made love with so passionately.

Dressed in a clean pair of shorts and a pale-pink T-shirt, she left the bathroom. She stopped at the dresser and grabbed her hairbrush and began to brush the tangles from her wet hair.

She stroked the brush several times through her hair, then paused as she heard a strange noise. She stood still for a moment, trying to identify the odd rattling noise. It seemed to be coming from some-place behind her.

Gazing into the mirror, she looked past her reflection and studied the room. Nothing looked amiss. Certainly she was alone. So what on earth was making that weird noise?

She turned away from the mirror and froze as her gaze fell to the bed. There, coiled in the center, a huge rattlesnake eyed her with wary intent, its rattle sending a warning of imminent attack.

For a moment Lilly couldn't breathe, was afraid that in taking a single breath she would force the snake to spring toward her. Ice-cold fear shimmied up her spine as she stared at the serpent in horror.

She had no idea how it had gotten on her bed, and at the moment didn't care how it had gotten there, she simply wanted it gone.

It felt as if time stood still. Long, torturous moments passed as Lilly remained frozen in place.

Not knowing what else to do, still afraid of moving a muscle, Lilly opened her mouth and released the scream that had been momentarily trapped inside her. The snake coiled tightly, rattling frantically, and Lilly screamed again.

The door to her bedroom burst open and Ned Sayville flew in. ''Wha...''

In an instant he saw the problem. He froze next to Lilly. ''Give me your shoe,'' he said, not taking his gaze off the snake.

''My what?'' she whispered.

''Your shoe...your sandal.'' He stretched out his

hand. The snake's rattle seemed so loud now it filled the entire room with the ominous sound.

Lilly raised her foot behind her and grabbed her sandal, then handed it to Ned. She held her breath and watched in horror as he approached the bed. "Ned...wait..."

"Shhh, I know what I'm doing," he said, then jabbed the sandal toward the snake.

Instantly it struck, sinking its mouth into the foam rubber of the shoe, and at the same time Ned grabbed it around the back of its neck and head and pulled it up off her bed. Her sandal fell to the floor.

"It's all right now," Ned said.

Lilly gasped in relief and followed him as he carried it down the stairs and out the front door, where they met Matthew and several other ranch hands rushing toward the house.

"What the hell?" Matthew exclaimed.

"It was on her bed," Ned explained. He walked the snake some distance from the house, then bent down and released it.

"Are you all right?" Matthew asked, his gaze fierce and intent on her.

She hesitated a moment, then nodded, wishing he would take her in his arms and pull her tight against his broad, safe chest. But he didn't.

"What happened?" he asked Ned as the man returned to the crowd that had gathered.

Ned shrugged. "I was working out here pulling weeds like you told me to, and I heard her scream." He looked at Matthew worriedly. "I didn't think...I just ran inside."

"No, it's fine, Ned," Matthew reassured him, and clapped him on the back. Ned visibly relaxed.

"I'd just like to know how a snake got all the way upstairs," Ned said thoughtfully.

"So would I." Lilly fought off a shiver, then walked over and took Ned's hands in hers. "Thank you, Ned. That was a very brave thing you did." She released his hands.

His cheeks flushed red. "Ah, it wasn't nothing...just a little old snake."

"You didn't see anyone go into the house?" Matthew asked him.

"No, but I'd only been here a minute or two before I heard her scream," Ned explained. He shot a shy smile to Lilly. "She's got a good set of lungs on her."

Lilly laughed, aware of the sound of a touch of hysteria in her laughter.

"All right, everyone back to work," Matthew said to the workers who were milling around. He turned and looked at Lilly. "We'd better go up and check your room, make sure there are no other surprises there."

"All right." With one more grateful look at Ned, Lilly followed Matthew back into the house and up the stairs to her bedroom.

They searched under her bed, in the closet, beneath the dresser, looking for anything that didn't belong there, for anything that might be a threat. But they found nothing.

"Are you sure you're okay?" he asked, a touch of gentle concern in his voice.

She nodded and pulled the bedspread from the bed. "I'm fine. It was just frightening to see that…that…thing on the bed when I finished taking my shower."

"You don't know if it was there before you took your shower?"

She shook her head and held the spread against her chest. "It might have been there. I don't know. I didn't pay any attention." She looked down at the spread in her arms. "I have to wash this. I can't imagine crawling beneath it tonight until it has been washed."

Matthew took the spread from her. "I'll carry this downstairs," he said.

Together they walked back down the stairs, neither of them saying a word. When they reached the kitchen, Matthew went into the laundry room as Lilly sank down into a chair at the table.

Even though the threat was gone, her legs felt shaky, and fear still swirled around inside her. She closed her eyes, imagining what might have happened if she hadn't seen the snake…if she'd backed up closer to the bed, unaware of the danger there.

She heard the sound of the washing machine being started, then Matthew returned to the kitchen. Instead of joining her at the table, he leaned against the island, his eyes dark and fathomless.

"I'll get to the bottom of this, Lilly. I promise you," he said.

She nodded. She knew his sentiments were right, but she also knew it was probably a promise he wouldn't be able to keep. Nobody had seen anything

unusual. Nobody had seen anyone creeping into the
house carrying a snake.

Why would somebody want to put a rattlesnake
in her bedroom? Who might want to harm her? And
for God's sake why?

"We've always been pretty lax around here at
locking things up," Matthew said. "That's going to
change. I'll go into town this evening and get a couple of extra house keys made for you and Clara.
From now on whenever you leave the house, lock
it up." His gaze lingered on her for a long moment.
"Are you sure you're okay?"

"I'm fine. Just a little shaky. Seeing that snake
on my bed was the most terrifying moment I think
I've ever had."

He continued to look at her, then sighed and raked
a hand through his hair in a gesture of frustration
that had become familiar to her. "Lilly...about yesterday...I'm sorry if I was a little rough on you."

"No, I'm sorry." Pleasure swept through her at
his apology. "I can be a real pain sometimes. I pick
and prod into things that aren't my business and for
that I apologize to you."

A whisper of a smile lifted the corners of his lips.
"You can be a real pain, but I know you mean
well."

"I do," she said honestly. And there was so much
more she wanted to say. She wanted to tell him that
she cared about him, that there was a small part of
her that was afraid for him...afraid that the anger
inside him would eventually consume him.

But she said none of that, knew speaking of those

things would be the worst possible thing she could do in the wake of the olive branch he seemed to be tentatively offering her.

He shoved off the island. "I'm heading back out to talk to everyone and see if anyone saw anything that might give us some answers."

"Will you be here for supper?"

"Don't plan on me," he replied. "I'm not sure how long it will take me in town. I'm going to meet with Judd Stevens and give him some paperwork. I'll just grab something to eat at the café."

"Judd Stevens?"

"He's a private investigator. I'm having him check the information on the job applications of the people who work here."

"Then I guess I'll see you sometime tomorrow," she said.

He nodded again, then left her alone in the kitchen.

Although she'd been hungry when she'd come back to the house, her appetite had fled in the wake of the trauma. She fixed herself a glass of iced tea, then sat at the table and waited for the washing machine to finish up its load.

When the washing machine was done, she put the bedspread in the dryer, then moved to the front porch and sat down just in time to see Matthew's pickup pulling away from the ranch and heading into town.

For a moment she wished he'd asked her to ride along. The afternoon and evening hours stretched out empty before her.

She sat on the porch until the bedspread was dry, then took it back upstairs and remade the bed. By that time her appetite had reawakened and she returned to the kitchen and fixed herself lunch.

After cleaning up her lunch dishes, she carefully locked up the house and went to her aunt's cottage, deciding she would spend the afternoon and evening hours there until Matthew returned from town.

The afternoon sped by pleasantly. The two women took a walk and visited with some of the workers. They ate chicken casserole for dinner, then turned on the television to watch until bedtime.

But as the sitcoms played, Lilly found her thoughts far away from the canned laughter and hokey situations. Instead she found herself once again thinking about Matthew...and his siblings...and their father.

"Aunt Clara?"

"Yes, dear?" Clara sat on the end of the sofa, her fingers nimbly working two knitting needles and a ball of yarn in pastel green and yellow. She was knitting a baby blanket for April, Mark's wife.

"Tell me about Uncle Adam," Lilly said.

Clara's fingers halted their movements and she looked at Lilly in surprise. "What do you want to know about him?"

"What kind of a man was he?"

Clara began to work the yarn again, a frown creasing her forehead as she looked at her fingers. "He was an unhappy boy who grew into an unhappy man. We were never close, Adam and I." She looked back at Lilly. "Why are you asking about Adam? What brought all this on?"

"Did you know he was abusive to his children?" Lilly watched the shock sweep over Clara's features and had her answer.

"Who told you that?" she asked as her hands dropped to her lap.

"Matthew. And Johnna. They said he was a monster," she said softly.

Clara's frown deepened, and she released a deep, audible sigh. "I knew he was harsh with the children."

"According to them, it was more than harsh. He beat them both physically and emotionally."

"Oh, my. Those poor babies. You know, I tried to help Adam when Leah first died. I came out here and told him I'd help with those poor motherless babies. But he sent me away, told me he was perfectly capable of raising his own."

She set her knitting aside and stared at the television for a long moment. "I came to visit when I could," she said, not looking at Lilly. "Everything seemed to be all right. Of course, the children were the best behaved I'd ever seen, but I worried so."

Lilly left her chair and went to the sofa and sat down next to Clara. The last thing she had wanted to do when she'd begun this conversation was cause Clara pain, and yet she saw the heartache shining from Clara's eyes.

"I called Social Services a couple of times, insisted they check on the children." Clara continued. "I needed to do it for my own peace of mind."

"And what happened?" Lilly asked curiously.

Clara shrugged her plump shoulders. "Nothing. I was told that Adam Delaney was a fine, upstanding citizen who was raising his children with a firm but loving hand. But I worried that they were white-washing things."

"What do you mean?"

Clara's blue eyes were troubled as she gazed at Lilly. "Adam was a wealthy rancher with plenty of power in this county. When he turned this place into a dude ranch, his power increased. He brought commerce to the town, and I'm sure nobody wanted to step on his toes."

She sighed. "When they were little, I shouldn't have let Adam bully me into staying away. I should have known Adam would raise his children the way our father raised us, but I'd hoped he'd do better, be better."

"Your father was abusive?" Lilly asked, and took Clara's hand in hers as the old woman nodded.

Clara smiled and squeezed Lilly's hand. "Yes, he was mean and abusive, but what are you going to do? You don't pick your parents. You, of all people should know that."

They rarely spoke of Lilly's real parents, and at the thought of them a faint band of pain wrapped around Lilly's heart. She leaned forward and kissed Clara on her cheek. "I think God knew what he was doing when he brought us together," she said.

"I know he did," Clara replied, her eyes shining bright with the love that had sustained Lilly through the years.

That was the end of their conversation about parents and Adam Delaney, but that didn't stop the thoughts from whirling around in Lilly's head.

So Adam Delaney had been an abused child who had become an abusive parent. It was a tragic story replayed far too often, a cycle of pain.

Lilly's heart ached with Matthew's pain of growing up the way he had, but the little bit of information Clara had shared with her did nothing to help her understand Matthew's self-imposed isolation or the anger that seemed to be such a part of him.

It was almost nine o'clock when Lilly heard the sound of Matthew's pickup returning home. She and Clara had shut off the television an hour before and had moved to sit on the porch of the small cottage.

"I'd better get to the house before Matthew locks me out for the night," she said as she stood.

"Yes, and it's getting close to my own bedtime," Clara said, also rising. She leaned forward and gave Lilly a kiss on the cheek. "You sleep well, dear."

"And you," Lilly returned. Then, murmuring a good-night, she left the cottage and headed for the house.

She walked into the house and met Matthew coming down the stairs. "I knocked on your door and realized when there was no answer that you weren't here," he said.

"I spent the afternoon and evening with Aunt Clara," she explained.

He pulled a key from his pocket and handed it to her. "I've got one for Clara, too. I'll give it to her tomorrow."

"All right," she said. He looked tired, the lines of stress cutting deeper than usual around his eyes. She wanted to reach up and stroke those lines, but she couldn't forget that the last time she'd reached out to touch him, he'd grabbed her arm as if she were flames that burned him.

"You look tired," she observed.

"I am." He swept a hand through his hair. "So if you'll excuse me, I'll just lock up and go to bed."

"Good night, Matthew," Lilly murmured, then as he swept past her to lock the door, she walked slowly up the stairs wishing there was something she could say, something she could do to break through the wall he kept so firmly erected around himself.

She opened the door to her bedroom and a small gasp escaped her as she saw what was in the center of her bed. A rose. A single, long-stemmed red rose.

She picked it up and drew the scarlet blossom to her nose, breathing in its sweet, heady fragrance.

Matthew.

Perhaps she had in some way broken through his wall after all. She undressed and pulled on her night-gown, every nerve in her body crying out for a touch…his touch.

He'd bought her a rose. The gesture thrilled her, and the single, long-stemmed rose touched her more deeply than any flower that had ever been bought for her.

Was it an invitation? A prelude to romance? Her heart thudded with the possibility. Why else would he have bought it for her?

Sweet anticipation rushed through her as she

thought of being held in his arms once again. Decision made, she crept from her bedroom and down the stairs to Matthew's room.

The door to the master bedroom was opened slightly and she knocked, then entered. Immediately she heard the sound of water running in the adjoining room and realized he was in the shower.

This room, the master suite, was huge. Decorated in navy blue and deep maroon, it was bold and masculine and the entire room smelled of Matthew.

With her heart pounding in anticipation, she sat down on the edge of the king-size bed, hoping, praying she hadn't mistaken his intentions.

Chapter 8

Matthew stood beneath the shower, welcoming the hot spray of water that beat against his knotted muscles. He felt as if they were all under siege by an unknown enemy. The problem with unknown enemies was that it was impossible to launch a defense, impossible to know what to expect next.

The idea that somebody had sneaked into the house, silently stolen up the stairs and placed a rattlesnake in the middle of Lilly's bed both enraged him and filled him with gut-twisting fear.

What if she hadn't seen the snake in time? What if she had sat on the edge of the bed? The snake would have struck and the result might have been deadly.

As he thought of Lilly lying in a hospital bed clinging to life, her eyes glazed and empty, his heart snarled into a thousand knots.

He grabbed the bar of soap and stuck his head beneath the steamy spray. Lathering up, he thought of the frustrating hours he'd spent in town.

The first thing he had done was go to the hardware store to get keys made. It had galled him that suddenly his house was no longer the safe haven it had been, that somebody had impinged on his sense of security.

Inferno had always been the kind of place where doors weren't locked and people weren't afraid. Matthew couldn't remember the last time he'd locked up the house. It had always been open to welcome friends, family and guests who might venture inside.

After the hardware store, he'd gone to the sheriff's office, where he'd told Jeffrey Broder about the snake. He had no illusions that Jeffrey would get to the bottom of things. Hell, he had no illusions about himself getting to the bottom of what was going on around the ranch.

He rinsed off the soap, then turned off the shower and stepped out. He grabbed a large towel, dried off, then wrapped the towel around his waist and left the bathroom.

She was the first thing he saw in his room. Lilly sat on the edge of his bed, illuminated by the glow of the lamp on his bedside stand.

The pale-pink nightgown did little to hide the thrust of her breasts, and through the thinness of the material he could see the faint dark circles of her nipples. Instantly his body reacted, and he was grateful for the towel around him.

"Lilly, what are you doing in here?"

She stood and approached him, her eyes shining with an evocative light that made his breath catch in his throat. She said not a word, but instead wound her arms around his neck and pressed herself against him.

Despite the fact that he didn't want this, told himself he couldn't want her, his arms enfolded her. She leaned her head against his chest, and he bent his head to smell her hair, the fragrant scent shooting rich hot desire through him.

He closed his eyes, allowing her nearness to suffuse him with warmth, with a pleasure so intense it was almost frightening.

"I wanted you to hold me this afternoon." Her voice was muffled against his chest, her breath a sweet tease of warmth. "I needed to be held by you."

Matthew reached up and stroked her hair, recognizing now the need that had driven her to him. It was nothing more than residual fear, a delayed reaction from the trauma of finding a deadly snake in her bed.

"Lilly..." He attempted to pull away from her, needing to distance himself before they made another mistake, before he lost control and made love to her once again. But he found it impossible to untangle himself. His arms ignored his head's wish, and his feet stubbornly refused to move backward and away from her.

For a long moment she stood in his arms, her face pressed against his bare chest, her breath warm against his skin. When he thought he could not bear the closeness another moment, she raised her head and looked up at him, a smile curving her sweet, kissable lips.

"Thank you for the rose," she said.

Matthew froze, any and all thoughts of physical pleasure blown away by her words. "The rose?"

Shock radiated over her features as she heard the questioning tone of his voice. "You didn't get me a long-stemmed red rose and leave it on my bed?"

She stepped away from him and instead wrapped her arms around herself, still holding his gaze. The shock on her features was replaced by fear.

"A snake and now a rose? What in the hell is going on?" Matthew exclaimed as he grabbed a clean pair of jeans from a drawer. He pulled them on under his towel, then threw the towel to the floor of the bathroom.

When he turned back to look at Lilly, she had sunk to the edge of the bed, as if her legs would no longer hold her upright. He sat next to her and worried a hand through his hair. "Did you lock up everything when you left here to go to Clara's for the evening?" he asked.

She nodded. "I made sure both the front door and the back door were locked up tight."

He frowned. "Then how did somebody get in here to put that rose on the bed?"

Her eyes appeared larger than usual, more luminous as she held his gaze. "There's really only two ways. Either somebody sneaked in while I was in the kitchen having lunch, or somebody was inside the house the whole time.''

She reached out for his hand, and he grabbed hold of hers, instinctively knowing she needed the connection. Her fingers were icy cold, attesting to the fear that darkened her eyes.

''I don't understand this. I don't understand any of it. Why would somebody put a snake on my bed, then wait and place a rose there? It doesn't make any sense.''

''No, it doesn't,'' he agreed. Scattered thoughts whirled around in his head as he tried to make sense of the senseless. ''The only thing I know for sure is that nothing out of the ordinary happened until you showed up here.''

She snatched her hand from his. ''Are you trying to say that this is all my fault?''

''No, of course not,'' he protested. ''I'm just thinking out loud.'' He frowned thoughtfully and reached for her hand once again. ''I thought what was happening around here was about me—the vandalized rooms, the stolen lumber. But now we have to think about the fact that somehow what is happening here might be about you.''

She released his hand and stood. ''But that's not possible. How could any of this be about me? I don't know anyone here, there's nothing about me that could make all of this happen.''

With the illumination of the lamp behind her, her nightgown was nearly transparent. Matthew averted his gaze from her, finding it difficult to think with the allure of her near nakedness so apparent.

''I don't know what to think,'' he replied. ''But it's something we have to consider.'' He hesitated a moment, then looked at her once again. ''Why did you take a leave from your job, Lilly?''

She blinked in surprise and averted her gaze from him. ''That has nothing to do with what's going on here and now.''

Matthew had never seen Lilly with secrets in her eyes, but that's exactly what he saw now. He rose and approached where she stood. ''Tell me, Lilly,'' he said. ''If there's nothing to it, then we can dismiss it from our thoughts.''

''I only wish I could dismiss it from my thoughts,'' she replied. Her voice held a piercing ache of sadness that touched a chord deep inside him.

She looked around the room, her eyes darting here and there as if seeking some sort of respite, some sort of escape. Then her gaze locked with his and she sighed and once again wrapped her arms around herself. ''I lost a student.''

He placed his hands on her shoulders, sensing she once again needed his touch. ''What do you mean?''

Her beautiful blue eyes suddenly brimmed with sparkling tears. ''His name was Danny Carpenter. He was a senior, mere weeks from graduation.''

''You were counseling him?'' Matthew guessed.

She nodded, and silvery trails of tears slid down her cheeks. ''He was an excellent student, but he wasn't sure if he wanted to go to college or not and there had been some incidents...some fights that were out of character for him. Some of his teachers were worried about him and so he was sent to me.''

She swiped her tears with the tip of her fingers. ''I met with him for several weeks and spoke to his parents about getting him into see a psychologist. I knew he was troubled...I could see it in his eyes, but I thought I was making progress with him.''

The tears fell faster now, far faster than her fingers could wipe them away. The pain that radiated from her eyes hurt inside his heart. He had never seen Lilly cry before. He'd never seen her filled with such deep despair.

Tenderly he pulled her back into his arms, and once again she buried her face in his chest. ''The last time I saw him, he seemed to be doing better. He told me he'd decided on a college and he seemed happier than I'd ever seen him.''

The tears that had silently coursed down her cheeks now transformed into silent sobs that shook her shoulders. He held her more tightly, as if to absorb her pain.

''He left my office and went home and took an overdose of pills.'' The words came with difficulty through the sobs. ''He killed himself, Matthew. That poor boy took his own life.''

''You couldn't have known,'' Matthew said, stroking her hair as she cried her heartache into his chest. ''You couldn't have done anything differently.''

''But I should have known,'' she protested, and raised her head to look at him. ''I saw the darkness in his eyes...darkness just like—'' She broke off and stepped away from him. "Anyway, now you know why I took some time off. It can't have anything to do with what's happening here."

Once again she sat on the edge of the bed and wiped her cheeks as if her tears embarrassed her. He sat next to her and put an arm around her shoulder, pulling her against him in an effort to comfort her.

"You can't save the world, Lilly," he said softly. She leaned into him as her sobs slowly subsided.

"I know," she replied. "But I wanted to save him," she added wistfully. She heaved a deep sigh. "He had so much potential, but I guess life was just too painful for him."

Matthew knew that kind of pain. There had been times in his life when he'd believed death would have been a welcome release from that pain. But thoughts of self-destruction had been fleeting, cast aside beneath the determination to survive his old man, thrive in spite of Adam Delaney.

"And this still doesn't tell us who left that rose on my bed and why," she said.

Matthew wished he had bought her that rose. He thought of the shine in her eyes, the curve of her lips when she'd believed the rose had been a gift from him.

Her eyes were now red-rimmed with tears. She wore exhaustion like a heavy robe. It weighed down her shoulders and pulled at her features.

"Come on," he said and stood. He held out a hand to her. "You're tired."

She placed her hand in his and stood. Together they left his bedroom and walked up the stairs to her room. The rose was still in the center of her bed, a scarlet mystery that fired a deep apprehension in him.

She picked it up and tore it apart, then carried the petals and stem to the trash can. Matthew pulled down the bedspread and gestured her into the bed, the apprehension quieting as desire reawakened in him.

As she crawled in beneath the sheets, he recognized that there was nothing more he'd like to do than crawl in beside her, make slow, sweet love to her and then hold her through the long hours of the night.

But in telling her about her student, she'd illuminated her reason for being attracted to him. She wanted…no, she needed to fix him. It was as if in fixing him she could somehow assuage her guilt over not being able to fix Danny.

"I'm going to double check your room," he said once she was in bed. She nodded, her tear-swollen eyes already half-closed with weariness.

He checked under the bed, in her closet and in the bathroom, making sure nobody was hiding anywhere, making sure nothing was amiss. Confident that everything was as it should be, he walked to the doorway. "Sweet dreams, Lilly," he said softly. She murmured something sleepily, and he quietly closed the door to her room.

With grim determination, Matthew went down to his study and got the revolver he kept in a locked drawer of his desk. After making sure it was loaded, he then checked the rest of the house, making sure no intruder was hidden within.

He looked in every room, every closet of the big house. He looked in every space and area that was big enough to hide somebody, the gun ready for a confrontation.

When he was certain the house was secure, he made certain the doors were locked tightly, then returned to his room. As he set the gun on his nightstand, a burst of rage fluttered through him, rage that some unknown entity had him sleeping with a gun next to his bed.

He peeled off his jeans and got into bed, his thoughts going back to Lilly. He'd never seen her with such pain in her eyes, never known her to shed a single tear. Her heartache over the student she had lost had resonated deep inside him.

He now recognized what drove her to pick and prod inside him, her talk about forgetting the past and letting go of his pain. She was driven by the trauma of Danny's death, and perhaps she believed that in healing Matthew she would somehow find salvation for herself.

Staring up at the ceiling, he thought of those moments when he'd held Lilly in his arms. She'd been so warm against him, stirring him not only on a physical level, but on a mental one as well.

He'd wanted to take away her tears and replace them with laughter. He'd wanted to hear her ramble on about something inconsequential, see her features animated with life and spirit.

He frowned, listening to the solitary sound of his

own heartbeat. For the first time in his life he suspected that he wasn't just a man who chose to be alone. For the first time in his life Matthew faced the knowledge that he was a lonely man.

Lilly was surprised to discover that in telling Matthew about Danny, in crying tears of sadness, some of the pain inside her had dissipated. Oh, she would always have a certain amount of pain where thoughts of Danny were concerned, but the ache didn't seem as intense anymore.

As she made dinner the next day, she thought of those moments in Matthew's room, when he'd held her so tenderly as she'd cried.

She'd always suspected that Matthew had a deep well of tenderness, of gentleness inside him, and her suspicions had been right.

Of course, she still intended to leave here in a couple of days, right after Aunt Clara's tests were done. Experiencing Matthew at his most tender, at his most passionate had been wonderful, and it had also been more than a little frightening.

She was allowing him to get too close, to get into areas of her heart she'd always proclaimed off-limits. She couldn't afford to stay too much longer, couldn't afford to allow herself to fall in love with him.

Flipping the hamburgers, she dismissed the very idea that she could possibly fall in love with him. He was cold and authoritarian and refused to be a part of anything larger than himself.

He kept a cocoon of anger wrapped around him

most of the time and forbade anyone to get close to him. He was a difficult man, a complex one, and she wasn't sure he even had the capacity to love inside him.

The back door opened, and she turned to see him coming in. "Ah, just in time," she said. "I'm taking up the hamburgers now."

"Good, I'm starving." He went to the sink and washed his hands. "Can I do anything to help?"

"No, I've got it under control," she replied.

Within minutes they were seated together at the table, enjoying the simple meal she had prepared. "How did things go today?" she asked.

"Pretty good. The work on the old barn is coming right along."

Lilly smiled. "April will be so pleased. She has big plans for the barn."

"You spoke to her today?" he asked curiously.

She nodded. "She stopped by this afternoon to enlist my aid in helping to decorate the family room for the Halloween party. We're going to start on the decorations in the morning."

He shook his head. "If I know April she won't be satisfied until the whole place is decorated to the hilt."

"But she's a good social director?"

"The best we've ever had," he agreed.

"Will she continue to work after the baby is born?" Lilly asked curiously.

"That's one of the first things I asked her when I found out she was pregnant, and she indicated she plans on continuing as social director."

For a few minutes they ate in companionable silence. It was Lilly who finally spoke again. "April had an interesting take on the snake and the rose mystery," she said.

One of Matthew's dark brows rose quizzically. "What did she think?"

"She said maybe they were put there by two different people. Somebody put the snake in my room and maybe one of the workers felt bad for me and left the rose to make me feel better."

He frowned. "Well, that doesn't make me feel any better. All that would mean would be that there were two people skulking around in the house who didn't belong here."

"At least we got through today without any craziness happening," Lilly replied. "And I think that calls for a celebration."

"A celebration?" He eyed her warily.

She laughed. "Don't look so worried. I don't intend to suggest anything radical."

"Then what?" he asked.

"We made a deal that when the cottages were painted we'd wade in the creek. Why don't we clean up the dishes, saddle up a couple of horses and go out to the creek."

For a moment he hesitated, and she thought he would say no. But then a whisper of a smile curved his lips and he nodded his head. "Yeah, that sounds good."

"Great!" she exclaimed, looking forward to the evening to come.

It was just after seven when they took off on

horseback. Both of them were wearing shorts in anticipation of wading in the creek. They rode at a leisurely pace, chatting about the ranch and the changes that would take place when guests were once again present.

She couldn't help but notice that Matthew cut a dashing figure on horseback. He rode with the relaxed confidence of a man accustomed to being on horseback.

As they rode by the old barn, she tried not to think about what had taken place in the hayloft, but it was impossible to keep thoughts of their lovemaking at bay.

Her skin tingled with the memory of his touch, and a hunger to repeat the experience momentarily filled her up. She glanced over at him, wondering if he was having the same sort of thoughts as they passed the place of their tryst, but his features were unreadable and his eyes were focused on the landscape ahead of them.

Within minutes they were in the grove of trees that ran along the bank of the creek. They dismounted, then tied up their horses and sank down in the grass just at the edge of the slow-moving creek.

"This is one of my most favorite places on the ranch," she said as she kicked off her shoes.

"Yeah, it is nice," he agreed. "Lots of the guests come here to wade in the creek or sit in the shade."

He took off his shoes, then stood and grinned and held out his hand to her. "Come on, Lilly, put your money where your mouth is. I want to see just how deep you're willing to go.''

Laughing, she grabbed his hand and allowed him to lead her into the warm creek water.

He watched them from the cover of the trees, close enough that he could hear their voices but too distant to distinguish specific words. He'd watched them riding out together, looking far too cozy, and he'd followed on foot at a distance, his blood boiling.

Matthew Delaney was becoming a genuine threat. The tall cowboy was spending far too much time with Lilly, looking at her in a way that wasn't right, wasn't good.

He crouched behind a tree trunk and stroked the barrel of the high-powered rifle he held, his eyes narrowed as he watched the couple frolicking in the creek, their laughter riding the soft evening breeze.

They held hands as they walked in the water and he burned with the knowledge that Matthew was holding the hand that belonged to him.

With the dappled sunlight cascading through the trees and shining on Lilly, she looked so beautiful, the sight ached inside of him. His want was growing stronger. His need for her threatening to consume him.

He'd hoped that the vandalized cottages would keep Matthew busy for weeks. He'd never dreamed that the Delaneys would come together as a family and work together. From the gossip he'd heard, the Delaney siblings didn't like each other much, but that hadn't stopped them all from pitching in and cleaning up the mess in the cottages.

Lilly.

Her name sang through his veins and filled up his heart. He'd thought she would know by now—that they belonged together. He'd thought she would feel the magic when they were in the same area, look at him with that secret, knowing look. But she was distracted by Matthew.

Matthew. Damn him. He was definitely becoming a problem, and it was time to take care of the problem. With determined intent, he raised the rifle to his shoulder. A grim smile curved his lips as he brought Matthew into the gun sight.

''Bye-bye,'' he said softly and placed his finger on the trigger.

Chapter 9

Matthew had forgotten how much fun Lilly could be. Her laughter rode the evening air as they waded in the warm creek water. He found himself laughing along with her as she spoke of the merits of mud between the toes.

"I think it's very therapeutic," she said. "It's impossible to have any worries when mud is squishing between your toes."

He laughed again, realizing she was right. At least for the moment the worries of the ranch seemed distant and far away.

"And speaking of therapeutic," she continued with a warm smile. "Thank you for last night."

"For what?"

She shrugged and swept a foot through the water. "For being nice and supportive. I hadn't talked about Danny to anyone, and I guess I needed to talk about it.''

"You didn't even tell Clara?"

She shook her head. "I knew she'd worry about me, so I didn't tell her exactly why I'd taken the leave of absence from my work. I just told her I needed a little break.''

He nodded. He didn't want to think about why she had come to his room, knew that she had come to make love with him, her desire prompted by what she'd believed had been a romantic gesture by him.

He shot her a surreptitious glance. She looked as lovely as ever in a sleeveless pink blouse and cutoff jeans. When they'd started off, her dark hair had been pulled back at the nape of her neck, but now part of her hair had escaped the confines and looked charmingly disarrayed.

He jumped in surprise as water splashed on his face. Lilly laughed and scooped up another handful of water, intent on splashing him again.

"All right, now you're in for it," Matthew exclaimed as he wiped off his face. He bent down to fill his hands with water to return the favor.

A boom resounded and the high-pitched whine of a bullet whizzed just over his head. He grabbed Lilly and yanked her facedown to the protection of the bank.

"Are you all right?" He asked urgently, his heart banging against his rib cage.

"Yes, but what happened?"

"Somebody shot at us.'' His stomach clenched as

he realized had he not bent down at the moment he had, he'd probably be dead.

He raised his head in an attempt to peer over the bank, trying to discern exactly where the shooter might be hiding. Another boom resounded, and Matthew drew his head back, fear battling a rising anger.

Who the hell was out there? Hiding in the trees? Pinning them down with deadly intent? "I've got to get to my horse," he said, and gazed over in the distance where their horses were tied.

"No, Matthew, you can't," she cried. "You'll be shot if you try to do that." Fear radiated from her as she convulsively clutched his arm.

"Lilly, we can't just wait here like sitting ducks. I've got a gun in my saddlebag. At least with it we'll have some sort of a defense." He grabbed her hand and squeezed it, at the same time trying to offer her a reassuring smile.

Then, releasing her hand, he drew a deep breath and began to work his way across the bank. He kept his head down, aware that at any moment another shot could be fired and this one might find a target— him.

Silence surrounded him, an unnatural silence. Not a bird cried out, no animals scurried, not even an insect made a single buzz or click. The only sound was his own pounding heartbeat and his shallow, rapid breathing.

He would be most vulnerable when he left the bank to run to his horse. It was then that the shooter would have a perfect shot at him.

As he reached the area where he'd have to leave

the safety of the bank, he looked back at Lilly. She remained motionless against the ground, her head turned so she could watch his progress.

Even from this distance, he could see the fear that widened her eyes, see the tension that rippled through her body.

Was he the target, or was she? If he got shot making his way to the horse what would happen to Lilly? A new burst of fear exploded inside him. Not fear for himself but rather for her.

He tensed his body, ready to spring up and race for the horse, hoping he could get his gun out of the saddlebag before the shooter could draw a bead on him.

As he exploded from the bank, Lilly stood up and screamed. In the bright-pink blouse she made a perfect target as she yelled and waved her hands.

"Get down," he cried as he ran for the horses, wondering what in the hell she thought she was doing.

She fell back to the ground, and Matthew rushed to Thunder's side and plunged his hand into the saddlebag and pulled out his revolver.

Horse hooves drew his attention and he saw his brothers, Mark and Luke, riding fast in their direction. They both wore grim determination on their faces and carried shotguns in a position of readiness.

Matthew waved his arms, attempting to gesture for them to take cover, but they continued toward him. No shots exploded as they pulled up next to where he stood.

"We heard shots and thought somebody might be

in trouble," Luke said, his gaze sweeping over the area as he held his shotgun ready.

"We were in trouble," Matthew replied, also looking out in the distance to where he thought the shots had originated. "Somebody decided to take potshots at us."

Lilly joined them, her eyes still wide with residual fear. "Somebody tried to kill us," she said, her voice quavering with emotion.

"You know where the shots came from?" Mark asked.

Matthew pointed to a distant grove of trees. "Someplace over there," he said.

Mark looked at Luke. "Let's check it out." Together the two brothers rode off, and Matthew turned his attention to Lilly.

"What in the hell were you thinking? Standing up and screaming like that?" he yelled.

Suddenly he wanted to take her by the shoulders and shake her. He wanted to grab her and pull her against him, assure himself that she was all right.

"I was acting as a diversion," she replied. "I was trying to draw the fire from you."

"Dear God, Lilly, you could have been killed."

She averted her gaze from him. "I didn't want you to get killed," she replied softly.

Matthew stared at her for a long moment, awed by the sacrifice she'd been willing to make for him. She'd put herself in the line of fire in order to help him.

Nobody had ever done anything like that for him in his entire life. He didn't know how to reply and was saved from having to by the return of Luke and Mark.

"Somebody was there," Luke said and in one graceful movement dismounted his horse. "The brush next to one of the trees is broken and the grass is tamped down. But there's nothing there to indicate who it was."

"Or why they would be firing shots at you," Mark added with a deep frown. "This is serious stuff, Matthew."

"I know." Matthew swiped his hand through his hair. "Let's get out of here."

Gone was the pleasure of the evening, the laughter and the relaxation. In its place was the rise of the rage that was so familiar to him.

They were all silent on the ride back to the stables. Again Matthew found himself trying to make sense of what had just happened, trying to figure out why somebody would want to harm either him or Lilly.

When he'd encouraged her to tell him about why she had taken a leave of absence from her work, he'd hoped the reason might shed light onto what was happening here and now. But in Danny's tragedy he had found nothing to tie in to the suspicious happenings here.

"The rose that was left on your bed confuses me," Matthew said to Lilly as they unsaddled the horses.

"What rose?" Although it was Luke who spoke, both Luke and Mark looked at Matthew curiously.

He explained to them about the events of the af-

ternoon before, the snake found in Lilly's room, then
the appearance of the rose in the center of her bed.

"What's confusing is that everything else that has
happened around here has been threatening. The
rose just doesn't seem to fit with everything else."

"Maybe the rose doesn't have anything to do
with any of the other incidents," Luke replied.
"Maybe Lilly has a secret admirer who tried to
make her feel better after the snake thing."

A secret admirer? Matthew wasn't sure why, but
the idea didn't sit well with him. He didn't like the
idea of somebody yearning for Lilly, perhaps lusting
for her.

"I've never had a secret admirer before," Lilly
replied. "And I'm not sure I like it."

"Are you going to call Sheriff Broder?" Mark
asked.

Matthew frowned thoughtfully, then nodded.
"Yeah. I know Broder probably won't be able to
tell us who fired those shots, but there needs to be
a report made."

They finished with the horses, put them in the
appropriate stalls, then left the stables. Standing just
in front of the building, Matthew looked around,
wondering if the shooter was someplace nearby,
watching…waiting for another opportunity.

He saw nobody. All the ranch help would have
either left for the day or returned to their cottages
for the night. There was no way to figure out who
might be the guilty party, just as there was no way
to be certain if the target of the shooter had been
him or Lilly.

"So what do we do now?" Mark asked.

"Hell if I know," Matthew replied, anger once again welling up inside him. He felt helpless, impotent in the face of uncertain danger, and he didn't like the feeling at all. "I guess the best that we can do is to be careful."

He turned to look at Lilly. "Don't go wandering off anywhere alone. In fact, it might be a good idea for you to stick close to the house."

"Aunt Clara has those tests at the hospital day after tomorrow," she reminded him. "I'll need to drive her into town for that."

"I'll drive you," Matthew said.

"What can we do?" Luke asked.

Again Matthew frowned. "I'm not sure there's anything you can do. I've hired Judd Stevens to do some checking into the backgrounds of everyone who is working for us, see if anyone is hiding anything we should know about."

"Smart move," Luke replied. "What about Jacob Tilley? We know he has a motive for revenge."

Weariness gripped Matthew. "I just don't know what to think," he admitted.

He glanced at Lilly, remembering when she'd jumped up and faced the possibility of being shot in order to divert the danger from him.

In that moment he had recognized that he was precariously close to falling in love with Lilliana Winstead. And this recognition filled him with more terror than the shots he had just faced from an unknown foe.

Excusing himself, he went in to contact Sheriff Broder.

She was in love with Matthew Delaney. Lilly had no idea how it had happened, couldn't understand how despite her resolve not to allow it to happen, it had.

Although she didn't know exactly when she had fallen in love with him, she knew the exact moment her own feelings had revealed themselves to her. It had been when the first bullet had soared just above his head.

In that instant, Lilly's love for Matthew had exploded inside her, stunning her. And the feelings she'd discovered hadn't changed overnight. Sleep hadn't come easily as she'd struggled to understand how this had happened.

Knowing she loved him and doing something about it were two different things. Loving Matthew had not changed her resolve to remain alone.

"Lilly, could you hand me that orange crepe paper?" April, Mark's wife, asked. April, Aunt Clara and Lilly were working to transform the family room into a spooky, yet festive, party area for the Halloween party.

"Sure." Lilly grabbed the crepe paper from the sofa and handed it to April, who was wrapping it around the frame of a gilded mirror.

"What we need is a ladder," Aunt Clara said. "That way we can string the crepe paper from the ceiling."

"I'll see if I can find somebody to get us a ladder," Lilly said.

She had noticed earlier that morning that there seemed to be more activity than usual outside. Workers hustled here and there readying things for the arrival of guests a mere week away.

Matthew had left early that morning to head out to the old barn and help with the renovations. Lilly didn't expect to see him again until this evening.

She spied Eddie and Ned working together in front of the stables. Harnesses, bridles and saddles were laid out across sawhorses, and the two men were busy oiling each piece of equipment.

"Hi, Eddie, Ned," she said as she approached them.

They both smiled at her and set aside the rags they were using for rubbing in the oil. "'Morning," Eddie replied.

"Hi, Lilly," Ned said.

"I was wondering if either one of you might know where I can find a ladder. We're decorating the family room for the Halloween party and could use one."

"I think I saw one in the closet in the stable," Eddie said.

"Why don't I get it for you and carry it over," Ned said.

"Oh, that would be wonderful," Lilly exclaimed and shot the man a warm smile.

As Eddie got back to work oiling a saddle, Ned disappeared into the stable and reappeared a moment later with a six-foot ladder.

"Perfect," Lilly said, and the two of them headed back to the house.

"So you're getting it all decorated for the party," Ned said as they walked.

"Yes. You are coming to the party, aren't you?" she asked.

"I wouldn't miss it," he replied, his brown eyes alight with pleasure. "Although I haven't figured out what kind of costume to wear yet. What about you? You got your costume ready?"

"I don't think I'm going to be here for the party," she replied, fighting the stab of sadness that pierced her heart as she thought of leaving this place, of leaving Matthew.

"Really? So you're heading back home soon?" he asked.

She nodded. "My aunt is having some medical tests run tomorrow, and I'll probably leave to go back to Dallas the next day or the day after."

"Well, it's a damn shame that you'll miss the festivities." They stepped up on the porch and Lilly held the front door so he could angle the ladder inside.

He carried it into the family room where April and Clara were waiting. "Anyplace is fine," Lilly said and watched as he propped it up against one wall. "Thank you, Ned."

"My pleasure," he replied, then with a nod of his head to them all, he turned and left.

"He seems like a nice young man," Aunt Clara said.

Lilly nodded, although she wondered if it had

been Ned who had stood in the trees the day before and tried to shoot them.

She had spent much of the night wondering who might want to harm her or Matthew. But no matter how often, no matter how fervently she'd turned it over in her mind, no answers had been forthcoming.

There was only one thing that was crystal clear in her mind, and that was the fact that she'd fallen in love with Matthew Delaney. And she didn't intend to do anything about that but run back to her home and her life in Dallas.

"Why don't we set up the ladder against that wall and I'll decorate the mantel," April said.

Lilly moved the ladder to where she wanted it, but stopped April from climbing up it. "How about I do the high decorating. After all, I'm not the one who is pregnant."

April laughed. "I'm not an invalid," she protested. "Even though Mark has certainly started to treat me like one."

Lilly smiled at her. "That's sweet."

April smiled, a smile that reflected the love she felt for her husband. "Yes, it is sweet," she agreed.

"It does my heart good to see Mark, Luke and Johnna all so happy with their spouses," Aunt Clara said from her perch on the edge of the sofa. She was working to put together a honeycomb table decoration.

"They're tough, the Delaneys," April replied. "All of them have a hard shell that tends to keep people at bay, but the people who manage to break through that shell are lucky, indeed."

These words of April's haunted Lilly as they continued to work. It was just after noon when Aunt Clara announced that she intended to make the three of them lunch, and she disappeared into the kitchen, leaving April and Lilly alone.

"Mark told me what happened yesterday evening," April said in a low voice.

"Thanks for not mentioning it in front of Aunt Clara," Lilly replied. "I don't want to worry her."

"You must have been terrified." April sat on the sofa where Aunt Clara had been moments earlier.

Lilly sat next to her. "No more terrified than you must have been when Jacob Tilley's father was going to kill you and Mark."

"Ah, so Matthew told you about that." Her green eyes darkened. "Yes, that was absolutely horrifying. Walter Tilley's henchmen locked us up in a root cellar in the old barn. They were about to kill us when Matthew, Luke and Johnna showed up to save the day."

She smiled. "But it wasn't all horrible. It was in that root cellar waiting for death that I realized just how much I love Mark."

A universal experience, Lilly thought to herself. Apparently, when faced with your own mortality you had the ability to see the emotions otherwise denied or evaded. Just as April had discovered her love for Mark when faced with imminent death, so had Lilly discovered her love for Matthew when their lives had been threatened.

April reached out and touched the back of Lilly's hand. "You're in love with Matthew, aren't you?"

An instantaneous denial sprang to Lilly's lips but refused to take the form of a verbal reply. She looked down at her hands, then back at April. "I care about Matthew...deeply, but—"

"But he's a difficult man to love," April said. "They all are difficult to love. You have to get through lots of layers of protection to get to the core of each of the Delaneys." April shook her head. "Their father really did a number on them."

"But Mark and Luke and Johnna all have managed to put their childhood and their pain in the past. I don't think Matthew has managed to do that. He seems so filled with...with anger."

A crash from the kitchen halted the conversation. "Aunt Clara? Are you all right?" Lilly called.

There was no reply.

Lilly jumped up from the sofa, a sudden sense of dread rocketing through her. "Aunt Clara?" she cried out again, then raced for the kitchen, her heart banging frantically.

April followed behind Lilly, and as they entered the kitchen, both of them cried out in alarm as they saw the old woman crumpled on the floor, a broken plate nearby.

Terror shot through Lilly as she saw the woman she loved clutching her chest, pain torturing her features into a mask of fear.

"My heart," Clara gasped breathlessly. "I-it's my heart."

"Should I call for an ambulance?" April asked frantically.

Lilly made a split-second decision. "No, there's

no time. Just get a couple of men to help me carry her to my car,'' Lilly replied, praying that she was making the right decision. ''I've got to get her to the hospital.'' Before the words were completely out of her mouth, April had left the kitchen.

''Hang on, Aunt Clara,'' Lilly exclaimed and grabbed Clara's hand. ''We're going to get you help. You just hang on.''

It took precious minutes for Eddie and Ned to carry Clara out to Lilly's car and gently deposit her in the back seat.

''Want me to go with you?'' April asked.

Lilly started the engine with a roar. ''No. Just tell Matthew we'll be at the hospital.'' Without waiting for April's acknowledgment, Lilly yanked the car into gear and took off.

As she heard Aunt Clara's gasping breaths and moans of pain, Lilly felt as if she were having a heart attack, so deep was the pain and fear that coursed through her.

''Hang on, Aunt Clara,'' she said, trying to keep the panic, the terror out of her voice. ''Everything is going to be all right. Just try to relax and keep breathing.''

Lilly drove like a NASCAR racer, grateful that she encountered little traffic between the ranch and the hospital. With each moment that ticked by, she hoped she hadn't made a mistake in transporting the beloved woman herself.

She squealed to a halt at the emergency room entrance, grateful to see Dr. Howerton waiting for them.

''April called and told me you were coming,'' he said curtly as Aunt Clara was gently loaded on a gurney. ''I'll speak to you later in the waiting room.'' He didn't wait for her reply, but instead hurried after his patient, leaving Lilly alone outside the emergency room doors.

For a long moment Lilly stood staring at the doors, blinking back tears as she thought of the woman who had given her life meaning, the woman who had loved her when nobody else had.

Lilly couldn't imagine her life without Clara in it. Clara had been her anchor, the family Lilly had never had.

For the first time in her life, Lilly was sorry for the solitary lifestyle she'd chosen. Never had she needed somebody to lean on, somebody to hold her as much as she did at this moment.

Chapter 10

He found her in the waiting room, sitting alone in one of the cheap plastic chairs that lined the wall. Matthew had always thought of Lilly as energetic and vital, but at the moment she looked small and achingly vulnerable.

Her hands were folded in her lap and her eyes were closed, as if she were mentally sending prayers heavenward. "Lilly?" He spoke her name softly.

Her eyes opened and she launched herself up and out of the chair and directly into his arms. "Oh, Matthew," she cried, burrowing her face into his neck. "I'm so glad you're here."

As quickly as she'd thrown herself into his arms, she stepped away from him, her entire body emanating restless anxiety. "I've been waiting forever, but nobody will tell me anything. It's been too long. Something must be horribly wrong."

Matthew reached out and took her hands in his, then led her back to the chairs where he forced her to sit next to him and released her hands. "Lilly, it hasn't been that long," he said gently. "I came as soon as Eddie found me, which means it's been less than an hour."

She slumped back in the chair, her eyes haunted and dark. "It feels like I've been sitting here waiting to hear something for an entire lifetime."

"So what exactly happened? All April told me was that Clara had collapsed and you'd rushed her here."

"I don't know." She tucked her hair behind her ear, then refolded her hands in her lap. "April and I were in the family room and Aunt Clara had gone into the kitchen to see about some lunch. We heard a crash and ran in there and she was on the floor clutching her chest."

Tears brimmed in her eyes as she stared at him. "She has to be all right, Matthew. She's all I have. She's all I've ever had."

Matthew wanted to gather her into his arms, kiss away her tears, but at that moment Dr. Howerton entered the waiting room, his features grim as he faced them.

"How is she?" Lilly asked as she jumped up from her chair and faced the doctor.

"She had a heart attack, but we have her stabilized at the moment. We're running some tests on her now to give us some idea of what's going on with her heart. We'll have the results of those tests back within the next fifteen or twenty minutes."

"And then what?" Matthew asked.

"I've called in Dr. Winesburg from Tucson," the doctor explained. "He's a heart specialist and should be here within the hour. He'll make the decision on what happens once we have the test results back."

Dr. Howerton looked at Lilly sympathetically. "I'd suggest the two of you go over to the cafeteria, get some coffee or something to eat. It's going to be a while before we know exactly what's going on."

"We'll just wait here until Dr. Winesburg arrives," Lilly replied.

Dr. Howerton nodded. "We'll let you know what's going on as soon as we know." With these words he disappeared back through the door through which he had come.

Matthew and Lilly sat once again. "She'll be all right," Matthew said softly, trying to ease Lilly's fears. "She's strong and you got her here quickly."

She nodded, but he could tell his words had done nothing to assuage her worry and fear.

Minutes ticked by, agonizingly slow. They remained sitting side-by-side but not speaking. Matthew knew that nothing he could say would help. Only the doctor could erase the lines of tension from Lilly's face. Only the doctor could take away the dark fear in her lovely eyes.

It was nearly an hour later when Dr. Winesburg came into the waiting room. The heart specialist was an older man with kind blue eyes and a head full of white hair. He took Lilly's hands in his as he explained what they had found.

"Clara has a severe blockage of one of her arteries and we're going in to correct it."

"You mean surgery?" Lilly asked in alarm.

"Yes. Without immediate surgery Clara is a time bomb. Another heart attack is certain to happen unless we do something to widen the artery and get blood flowing once again." He released Lilly's hands.

"How dangerous is the surgery?" Lilly's voice trembled.

Dr. Winesburg smiled at her confidently. "It's a relatively simple procedure that I've done a thousand times before. She'll be in surgery for about two hours, and if all goes well she'll be able to go home within forty-eight hours."

"Can we see her?" Lilly asked.

"For just a few minutes. We'll be taking her in for surgery shortly. She's in room ten—through the doors and down the hall on your left."

Lilly reached for Matthew's hand, as if needing his support as they followed Dr. Wineburg's directions to Clara's room.

Matthew was shocked to see Clara lying so still, so pale in the large hospital bed that seemed to swallow her up. Lilly released his hand the moment they entered the room and rushed to Clara's side.

"Aunt Clara," she said softly, and Clara fluttered her eyes opened.

"Ah, my precious Lilly," Clara said. "I've given you a fright and I'm sorry."

"Shh, don't you dare apologize," Lilly exclaimed, and grabbed her hand.

"I guess they told you I'm going in for some surgery," Clara said.

"Yes, and we just came in to tell you that we love you and Dr. Winesburg told us everything is going to be fine," Lilly replied.

"Well, of course it is," Clara replied. "Of course, he's probably going to make me change my diet, cut out everything that tastes good."

She directed her gaze toward Matthew. "Dear Matthew, I'm so glad you're here." She held out a hand toward him.

He hesitated a moment, then stepped forward and allowed Clara to grab his hand. As he gazed down at her, he felt the stir of the old resentment he'd always felt for her...a resentment tempered for the first time by a wave of something frighteningly soft and strange. Her hand was dry, the skin feeling paper thin.

"Matthew...I'm sorry," Clara said, her gaze holding his intently. "Lilly told me about your father. I...I didn't know. Although I did worry... I did what I could, but it wasn't enough."

Matthew patted her hand, discomfited by the pain that radiated from her pale-blue eyes, a pain he knew had nothing to do with her physical condition.

Again he felt a reemergence of old resentment. Why hadn't she been able to see that they had desperately needed help? On her infrequent visits to the ranch, why hadn't she recognized that the Delaney children were in fear of their very lives?

He pulled his hand from hers and instead stuck his hands in his pockets. "Why didn't you visit more often?" he asked, trying to keep his voice evenly modulated despite the emotion that suddenly swam inside of him.

Clara closed her eyes for a long moment, and when she opened them once again there were tears sparkling in the pale blue depths. "Adam made it quite clear I was never welcome there." She paused a moment as if to catch her breath. "I...he frightened me. When we were young, he terrorized me so. He had such a mean streak in him."

He fought to hang on to his anger, needing it, but he couldn't. Any anger he might have once felt toward her was gone beneath the realization that she'd been as afraid of his father as all of them had been.

Why had he expected any more of her than he had of himself? Of other adults? She had been a woman all alone. Why had he thought it was her duty to take on a mean, hateful man?

"I wasn't sure there was anything wrong and I prayed that Adam was a good father," she continued. "I'd hoped he'd outgrown some of his meanness. But still I called Social Services several times. I wanted an investigation to set my own mind at ease."

Again she paused a moment, as if fighting for the energy to continue speaking. "Your father was a powerful man with influential friends. I'm sorry, Matthew, I'm so sorry for letting you and the others down."

"There's nothing to be sorry about," he said. He

realized it must have been hell growing up with an older brother like Adam Delaney. Her childhood had probably been no better than the Delaney children's.

"And all you need to focus on is getting well." With an impulse that surprised him, he leaned down and kissed her cheek, then stepped away from the bed.

At that moment the doctor came into the room and shooed them out. They returned to the waiting room and found it filled with Delaneys.

As Jerrod, Johnna, Mark, April, Luke and Abby all gathered around Lilly to learn about Clara's condition, Matthew stepped outside into the late-afternoon sunshine.

He walked over to a stone bench beneath a shade tree and sat down, his thoughts whirling.

The absence of any negative feelings for Clara surprised him. He'd wanted to make her a villain in his past, had needed somebody to blame for all the misery, all the pain they had endured. Aunt Clara had been an easy scapegoat, but she'd had no more power than the Delaney siblings had had.

She'd been a woman alone with no power or resources to help. If she'd attempted to step in the way of Adam, he would have crushed her beneath his heels.

He leaned forward and placed his head in his hands, hoping...praying that Clara would come through the surgery all right. She had to be all right, not so much for his sake, but for Lilly's, who loved her so.

"She's all I've ever had." Those were the words

Lilly had said to him, her eyes filled with unshed tears. They were words that confused him.

According to what his father had told him, Lilly had had a family until she was sixteen, when they had been killed in a tragic car accident. So how could Lilly believe that Clara was all she'd ever had. She'd had a family until she'd been sixteen.

"Matthew."

He looked up to see her approaching. She sat next to him, her gaze warm as she looked at him. "What are you doing out here?"

"Getting some air…thinking."

"I want to thank you," she said softly.

He frowned. "For what?"

"For being kind to Aunt Clara. For kissing her and letting her know you care."

He drew a deep breath. "I've blamed her for years for not rescuing us from my father."

"I have a feeling she underplayed the trauma of her childhood with your father."

Matthew nodded, knowing she was probably right. He looked at Lilly curiously. "You mentioned earlier that Clara was all you had…all you've ever had. But weren't you sixteen when your parents died?"

This time it was her turn to look surprised. "Don't you know how I met your aunt?"

"I have no idea. My father told me your parents had been killed in a car accident when you were sixteen and Clara took you in."

Lilly shook her head. "Aunt Clara was probably afraid to tell your father the truth."

"And what is the truth?"

"The truth is I met your aunt when I'd just turned sixteen and I tried to snatch her purse on the street outside her house."

She smiled at Matthew's stunned expression. "It's true. It's not something I'm particularly proud of, but I tried to grab her purse off her shoulder and run. Instead she grabbed hold of me and didn't let go."

"Why were you trying to steal her purse?" he asked incredulously.

She leaned back and gazed off into the distance, her smile fading. "Because I'd been living on the streets for three weeks and I was hungrier than I'd ever been in my life."

Matthew gazed at her in confusion. "I don't understand. Why were you living on the streets? Was this after your parents died in the accident?"

"No. That was just a story we made up," she replied. When she turned to look at him again her eyes were dark...haunted. "You aren't the only one who didn't have such a terrific childhood. My parents were drug addicts, and my early childhood was nothing but chaos and uncertainty."

Matthew was stunned by her disclosure.

"We moved around a lot because they often couldn't pay the rent," she continued. "We spent the summer that I was six living in our car." She tucked her hair behind her ear and leaned back against the trunk of the tree behind them. "My father was a carpenter. He'd try to stay clean, get work, but those periods never lasted very long."

"So what happened to them?" Matthew asked.

"I don't know. When I was eight years old we were living in a small apartment, and for the first time in a while life seemed sort of normal. I went to school one morning and when I came home that afternoon they were gone. They'd packed up and moved what little we owned and disappeared. A social worker was waiting for me."

She closed her eyes, and Matthew knew she was remembering that day. He reached out and took her hand in his, wanting to comfort the little girl she had been—a little girl thrown away by her parents.

Her fingers curled around his, and when she opened her eyes tears glistened there. "I was sure they'd be back, that it was all some sort of a horrible mistake. I insisted the social worker sit with me on the stoop of the apartment building and wait for my parents to return. We sat there all night long. When morning came I knew they weren't coming back for me."

Matthew placed an arm around her shoulder and drew her close against his side as she continued to speak. "I went into foster care after that. From the age of eight to sixteen I was in fourteen foster homes, then when I was sixteen I ran away."

"Where did you go?"

She shrugged and leaned her head against his shoulder. "The mean streets of Dallas. I found an abandoned building and stayed in it for three weeks. I've never been so dirty...so hungry and so scared in my life. The best thing I ever did was try to steal Aunt Clara's purse. She grabbed me by the arms, took me into her house and scrubbed and fed and loved me like I'd never been loved before.''

For a long moment neither of them spoke. Matthew silently tried to digest all that she had told him, imagining the pain of being abandoned and the fear of being alone. ''Why didn't you tell me all this years ago?'' he finally asked.

She sat up and looked him in the eyes. ''Probably for the same reasons you didn't tell me about your father. There are some things too painful to share at the time you are living them. That first summer that Aunt Clara brought me here, I was so afraid that I'd somehow do something to mess things up, I wasn't about to say anything to anyone about my past.''

It amazed him, how much he'd thought they had shared with each other on those summer days so long ago, and yet in reality how little they had shared. The integral parts of themselves, the essence of experiences that had made them the people they were they had jealously guarded, afraid to share.

''She has to be all right, Matthew,'' she said softly.

He squeezed her shoulder. ''She will be. She's tough.''

''I hope you're right. I need to get back inside,'' she said, although she didn't move from his side.

''I think I'll just sit out here for a little bit longer,'' he said. He wanted to digest what she'd told him about herself.

She pushed away from him and stood. ''I'll see you inside?''

He nodded, then watched her as she walked back

to the building and disappeared into the hospital doors. She positively amazed him. Now that he knew her background and the pain she had endured, her ability to love and her cheerful optimism awed him.

She seemed to carry no scars from her experience and he envied her that. But that didn't change the fact that the scars he carried were too deep to be healed, too toxic to be ignored.

He could love Lilly, if he allowed himself. But he'd promised himself a long time ago that he'd never, ever love a woman. And one thing Matthew never did...he never broke his promises.

It was just after ten when Lilly parked in front of the house. Matthew had left the hospital two hours earlier, when the doctor had told them that the surgery had gone fine and there had been no complications.

Lilly had stayed, and when Clara had been brought back into her room, she had sat next to her bedside, content to simply watch the old woman sleep peacefully.

The nurse had finally chased her out of the room, telling her to go home, get some sleep and come back in the morning. Realizing she was tired, Lilly had finally heeded the nurse's advice.

The front door was unlocked and she found Matthew sitting in the family room, a glass of brandy in his hand. "Ah, that looks wonderful," she said, and sank down in one of the wing chairs.

He stood and went over to the bar and poured her

a glass of the dark-amber liquid. "Here you are," he said.

"Thank you." She took a sip, then leaned her head back and swallowed.

"Everything okay?"

"Fine." She opened her eyes and took another sip. "The nurse finally kicked me out of Aunt Clara's room and told me to come home."

"Smart nurse," he observed as he sat on the edge of the sofa. "You look tired."

"It's been an incredibly long day." She kicked off her sandals and buried her toes in the thick carpeting, then took another sip of the smooth brandy. "Everything okay here?"

"Fine. Several of the workers have come by for news about Clara."

"That's nice. She's a special woman, Matthew. If you just give her a chance, she'll enrich your life."

He nodded, his features inscrutable. He finished his brandy, then carried the empty glass to the bar sink. "Did anyone say when Clara will be released from the hospital?"

"Day after tomorrow," Lilly replied. She took the last sip of her drink, then stood and carried her glass to the sink. "It's amazing, isn't it," she said as he took the glass from her. "That they did heart surgery today and she'll be released so quickly."

"Amazing," he agreed. His gaze lingered on her for a long moment. "Well, I guess I'll head to bed."

"Me, too," Lilly said, her pulse racing slightly. There had been something in his eyes when he'd looked at her that had shot adrenaline through her.

Matthew turned out the light in the family room and together they left and paused at the foot of the stairs where they would part ways to go to their separate bedrooms. A pale light drifted out of his bedroom providing just enough illumination for her to see his features.

"Matthew, thank you for being there for me today," she said. "I always feared that something would happen to Aunt Clara and I'd have to face it all alone. It was nice to have you and your family there with me."

"I'm glad I could be there for you." He reached out and touched a strand of her hair. Hunger. That's what she saw radiating from his eyes. A hunger for her.

Her throat went dry and her heartbeat accelerated. How she wanted to be held in his arms again. How she wanted to feel his touch burning her, setting her on fire. "Matthew?" His name whispered out of her.

"I want you, Lilly," he said, eyes blazing. "I want you in my bed, in my arms."

"I want that, too."

He pulled her to him and captured her lips with his, his hands tangling in her hair as his body pressed tightly against hers.

Lilly welcomed him, opening her mouth to him, arching against him in overwhelming need. He tasted of brandy and simmering passion, and she wanted to lose herself in him.

He broke the kiss only long enough to scoop her up in his arms, then he carried her into the bedroom and gently laid her on his bed.

As he undressed, she did the same, kicking off her shorts and taking off her blouse. There was no sense of shyness, no hesitancy inside her. Never had she felt so right about making love to a man.

When they were both naked, he rejoined her on the bed. He placed his hands on either side of her face and for a long moment gazed at her, his eyes filled with both a hunger and a sweet gentleness that stole her breath away.

"We're quite a pair, you and I," he said, his voice deeper, huskier than usual. "You've spent much of your life without a family and feeling all alone. I've spent much of my life with a family and feeling all alone." He kissed her lips softly, tenderly. "But at least for tonight, neither of us has to feel alone."

His words sought out and found a cold place she hadn't realized existed in her heart and warmed it with evocative heat.

Yes, she had spent most of her life feeling alone, but at the moment, with Matthew's arms wrapped tightly around her, the innate loneliness disappeared.

Then there was no time for further thought as he kissed her again and stroked down the length of her body with his slightly callused hands. His kiss was explosive, yet retained an underlying tenderness that wove its way straight to her heart.

The love she felt for Matthew, a love she'd fought against and tried to ignore, now expanded and rippled through her entire body and soul.

His touch was different this time from the first time they had made love. Gone was the frantic first-time frenzy, replaced by what seemed to be a languid savoring of her skin.

She moaned as his hands found her breasts, his thumbs raking over the turgid nipples and shooting sensation throughout her body.

"Oh, Lilly," he murmured softly. "You have made me half-insane over the past couple of days. All I've been able to think about is kissing you…making love to you."

"And I've wanted you," she replied breathlessly.

"The most difficult thing I've ever done in my life was take you back to your bedroom after you'd come in to thank me for that rose." He leaned his head down and captured the tip of one of her breasts in his mouth.

Any reply Lilly had been about to make was lost, just as she was lost to his touch, to his kiss, to him.

She splayed her fingers over the expanse of his broad back, enjoying the feel of his smooth skin and the play of muscles beneath. As his mouth moved from one breast to the other, she tangled her fingers in his thick hair, another moan escaping from her.

His touch ignited every nerve ending in her body, and it didn't take long for her to be enflamed with need. Still he took his time, languidly stroking her breasts, her stomach, her thighs, teasingly avoiding the place where she needed him most.

She didn't remain an uninvolved participant. She ran her hands across his chest, down his flat abdomen, then on to his muscled thighs, enjoying his quick catch of breath and the fire in his eyes as she teased him in return.

It didn't take long before the mutual teasing reached fever pitch and Lilly felt that if he didn't take complete possession of her immediately, she might die.

Apparently he was at the same place, for with a groan he rolled between her parted legs and entered her. As he moved his hips against hers, she cried out and shuddered as a climax swept through her.

He waited a moment, allowing her to catch her breath, then began to move again, beckoning her back up...up...to heights of pleasure she didn't even know existed.

As passion swallowed her whole, she had one final thought. How on earth was she going to walk away from this man? And yet she knew that's exactly what she had to do.

No!

He stood outside the bedroom window, the lamp on the nightstand illuminating the couple on the bed. He wanted to run away from the sight, and yet his feet walked him closer to the window. He wanted to close his eyes and banish the image of the two making love, and yet his eyes refused to look away.

Tremors shook his body...tremors of rage. How dare he? How dare he touch her so intimately. By all rights Matthew Delaney should be dead. Matthew should never have left that creek, should have fallen into the water, his blood spilling out of him from a rifle shot.

The watcher at the window balled his hands into fists. He should have taken the time to get off one final shot. Perhaps it would have been the one that hit his target. But he'd been aware that the sound of the two blasts he'd fired might draw attention, and so he had taken off, angered by his lack of success.

He didn't blame Lilly for this betrayal, knew she was an innocent who had been taken advantage of by the smooth, handsome cowboy. What he was watching take place in the bedroom was nothing short of rape, and hatred for Matthew Delaney coursed through him.

He had to get Lilly away from here. He had to get her away from Matthew. Once he had her alone, he could make her understand that they belonged together. He could make her understand that she was his.

Chapter 11

He felt as if he'd been starving for years and Lilly was a piece of life-sustaining bread. He felt as if he'd been thirsty for a lifetime and Lilly was a swallow of sweet, clean water.

Matthew knew in his heart that making love to her again was a mistake, but as he took possession of her, felt her surrounding him in heat, saw the glazed passion in her eyes, he also knew he couldn't not make love to her one last time.

After tonight he would stay away from her. After tonight he would never kiss her, never hold her, never make love to her again. But he had to have her tonight.

All afternoon he'd thought about what she'd shared with him, the pieces of her childhood that he hadn't known before. And for the first time in years he'd ached with somebody else's pain…he'd hurt with *her* pain.

He'd thought of the little girl she had been, sitting on a porch, waiting for her parents to return for her. He imagined her pain when the night had passed and they hadn't come back. He'd ached with the need to wrap her up in his arms and never let her go. He'd yearned to sweep away her past and rewrite it with happiness and love.

Once again he'd been awed by the fact that not only had she survived but she'd thrived, despite her past. And as he'd waited for her to return home from the hospital, a crazy need to hold her in his arms had filled him. The need had grown to fever pitch by the time she'd walked through the door.

She now moaned his name and he increased his rhythm, moving in and out of her warmth with the ancient tempo of lovers. Each and every movement shot overwhelming sensation through him.

He wanted this moment to last forever, yet felt himself building to fever pitch far too quickly. He slowed his pace in an effort to cool his fervor.

Each sweet little gasp, every precious deep moan she released, further stoked the flames of his desire. Her fingers raked across his back with each thrust he made and once again he increased his pace, unable to ignore the pounding pleasure of loving her.

He took possession of her mouth once again, their tongues battling in passionate warfare. He vaguely wondered if he would ever get the taste of her out of his mouth, the scent of her out of his nose, the memory of her out of his brain.

Faster and faster he moved with her, swept into a maelstrom of emotion so intense he could no longer think. He could only feel.

He felt his release building...building...and he cried out her name as he reached it, vaguely aware of her crying out, too.

Afterward he rolled to the side of her, both of them not speaking but rather waiting for their breathing to resume a more normal rate.

When his breathing was more regular, he propped himself up on an elbow and looked at her. She'd never looked as beautiful, with her hair tousled by his hands and her lips slightly swollen by his kisses.

He reached out a hand and trailed a finger down the side of her face. She reached up and grabbed his hand and brought it to her lips. She kissed the palm, then folded his fingers as if to capture the kiss.

"That's the way I give Aunt Clara kisses," she said, then frowned. "Matthew, she worried about you all when you were young. She was afraid for you all. She called Social Services several times on your father, but the reports came back that nothing was wrong, that you kids were all fine. And I got the impression from her that she would have visited more often, but your father bullied her."

Matthew sighed, not surprised by her words. He reached out and stroked a strand of her shiny hair. "I don't blame her anymore," he said thoughtfully. "Somehow seeing her in that hospital bed, hearing her tell me she was sorry, put it all into perspective for me. She was as helpless against my father as all of us were."

"You know what I always think about when I'm thinking of my childhood?" she asked, her eyes shining bright.

"What?"

"That old saying about that which doesn't kill you makes you strong."

He smiled at her. "Then you and I should be very strong."

"I think we are," she replied. "And there's nothing wrong with being strong as long as we don't fall into the trap of thinking we're so strong we don't need anyone else."

"You're doing it again," he said teasingly.

"What?"

"Counseling me."

She laughed, then sat up.

"What are you doing?" He wasn't finished holding her yet, wanted to hold her through the night and wake up at dawn with her in his arms.

"Going to the bathroom," she said. She started to get out of the bed, then suddenly rolled back against him. "Matthew, there's somebody outside the window," she said softly, her voice emanating urgency.

Matthew tensed, adrenaline rushing through him. "Are you sure?"

She nodded, her eyes radiating fear. "Positive."

Matthew reached over and grabbed the revolver from his nightstand, then got out of bed and grabbed his jeans. He moved with an enforced casualness. "I'll get us something to eat," he said loudly as he pulled on his jeans.

''Get something sweet,'' Lilly said, playing along.

Matthew nodded, and once he hit the doorway of the bedroom, he raced for the front door. The simmering anger that had always been a part of him burst into flame.

White-hot fury filled him as he exploded out the front door and raced around the house. The idea of somebody watching him and Lilly in their lovemaking, the idea that somebody had spied on them and seen her beautiful nakedness released a killing rage inside him.

Gun drawn, he turned the corner of the house and saw the window where Lilly had thought somebody had stood and peeked in on them. There was nobody there.

He eyed the general vicinity, making certain that nobody was hiding in the deep shadows of the house, then directed his gaze outward from the house, recognizing that there were all kinds of places to hide in the darkness of the night.

Moving closer to the window, his gun still ready, he saw where the brush had been tamped down by somebody standing there, and again rage soared through him.

It was an anger born in his childhood, bred in the events of the last couple of weeks and now sharpened by this latest violation. And in that anger was regret that he'd allowed himself to make love to Lilly once again.

He'd known better. It wasn't fair to her and it

wasn't fair to himself, to hold her, to kiss her, to love her with no intent to keep her in his life.

The realization of his own weakness where she was concerned merely served to stoke the fires of his fury higher. He checked around the perimeter of the house, then returned to the front door, where Lilly stood in the doorway now clad in a pale-pink robe.

"Did you find anyone?" she asked, fear visible in her eyes as he stepped inside and carefully locked the door behind him.

"No. Although the grass was crushed down just outside the window. Somebody was standing there recently." He switched the trigger lock on the gun, his rage still a seething entity inside him.

She wrapped her arms around herself and shivered. "Somebody watched us while we were making love."

"Well, whoever it was isn't watching anymore," he said grimly. "You should go on up to bed. I'm going to stay up for a while and make sure everything is all right around here."

He saw the disappointment that briefly swept over her features and knew she'd been anticipating a night spent in his bed, in his arms. "What's going on, Matthew? The rose...the gunshots and now this." She shivered once again.

He steeled himself against his own disappointment and instead embraced the anger that raged inside him. "I don't know. I wish to hell I did, but I don't. The best thing you can do right now is go to your room and lock the door. I don't need any distractions at the moment.''

His words and tone of voice were meant to inflict pain, and they hit the mark. He saw on her features the result of the hurtful words, and regret surged up inside him, momentarily usurping the anger.

''Okay.'' She belted her robe more tightly around her. ''Then I'll just say good-night.''

He watched as she went up the stairs, fighting the impulse to call her back, take her in his arms and apologize for his words. But he couldn't.

He recognized now that there was a magic between them that couldn't be denied. It had been there between them years ago when they'd been inexperienced teenagers, and it was still between them.

In another lifetime, in another destiny, they would have belonged together. But in this lifetime it was simply impossible.

It was family meeting night. Clara had been home from the hospital for two days, the Halloween party was to take place the next evening, and Matthew had never been as cold and as distant as he had been toward Lilly in the past three days since they had made love.

Not only had he been distant and cold, the anger that seemed to have simmered all along was now out in the open and exposed. He snapped at her and the workers, growled at his brothers and in-laws, and kept himself completely isolated from everyone.

The result of his bad mood stirred a surprising

anger in Lilly. How dare he blow so hot and cold, one minute being a gentle, passionate lover, then transforming into a miserable, angry bastard.

She didn't understand him, didn't understand the rage that seemed to be so much a part of him. But it frightened her. Oh, she wasn't afraid of him, rather she was afraid for him.

She knew now that he had an enormous capacity to love, that someplace deep inside him was a well of sweet tenderness, of caring and compassion. She couldn't love him if that wasn't so. But that capacity for loving was being smothered beneath the weight of his inexplicable rage.

"You're awfully quiet this evening," Clara said, breaking into Lilly's thoughts.

The two women were seated on her porch, waiting for the time when they would go to the main house for the family meeting.

"Just thinking," Lilly returned.

"About anything important?"

Lilly grinned at her aunt. "Don't you know that all my thoughts are important?" she teased, then sobered. "Actually, I've been thinking that maybe it's time I get back to Dallas. It's possible if I return fairly soon I can get a position in one of the schools for the remainder of the school year."

"You miss work?" Clara asked.

Lilly thought about it. The pain of losing Danny still pierced her heart, but she now had the distance to recognize she'd done everything in her power to help him.

There was nothing more she could have done. She

realized that some people were beyond help, their inner pain too intense. She suspected that Matthew was one of those people.

"Yes, I miss work," she finally replied, even though she was aware that it was a tiny white lie. What she missed was having something to think about, something to concentrate on other than Matthew Delaney.

"You know I'll hate to see you go," Clara said softly. She smiled at Lilly, the gentle, loving smile of a mother. "I still remember that first time I met you." Clara clucked her tongue against her teeth. "What a mess you were, so skinny and dirty, but I could see the beauty of your soul shining in those blue eyes of yours."

Lilly smiled and shook her head. "I still feel guilty about trying to steal your purse."

Clara waved her plump hands dismissively. "No need to feel guilty. You were a child trying to survive." Her gaze was warm as it lingered on Lilly. "I know you think I did something wonderful for you, taking you into my home and into my heart. But, Lilly, you did something wonderful for me. You filled all the empty spaces in my life, and not a day goes by that I don't thank the good Lord for bringing us together."

For a moment Lilly couldn't speak. Love and thankfulness filled her to capacity. "I give thanks every day, too," she finally managed to say.

Clara nodded. "Yes, I'll hate to see you go back to Dallas, but, I know it's selfish for me to want to keep you here with me."

Lilly reached for her hand and smiled. "There isn't a selfish bone in your body, but I do have to get back sooner or later." Lilly released her hand and continued, "Besides, it won't be too long before it's Christmastime and I'll be back here to visit."

"Christmas this year is going to be just lovely," Aunt Clara exclaimed, her face lit with anticipation. "We'll all be together, all of the Delaney children and their children. It's going to be just wonderful."

"Yes, it will be," Lilly replied. She only hoped that by Christmas her love for Matthew would have waned, become only a distant echo of memory that no longer hurt.

"And I don't want you going back to Dallas and worrying about me," Aunt Clara said. "You heard what Dr. Howerton told me. I'm fit as a fiddle and all I have to do is watch my diet, take those little pills for my cholesterol and I should be just fine."

"And that's a relief," Lilly said. She looked at her wristwatch. "We'd better head over to the house. Everyone should be arriving within the next fifteen minutes or so."

"Yes, and I want to put on the coffee and make some iced tea for everyone," Aunt Clara replied.

Together the two women left Clara's cottage and headed for the main house where they encountered Matthew in the foyer.

"Matthew, dear, I'm going to make some coffee and iced tea for the meeting tonight," Aunt Clara said. "Is there anything else you'd like me to do?"

"I don't know why you're going to all that trouble, it will just encourage them all to stay later than usual." He scowled. "I'll be in the office until everyone gets here." He turned and disappeared down the hallway into the office.

"Sometimes I think that boy needs a good spanking," Aunt Clara muttered under her breath. "I'll be in the kitchen," she said, and headed in that direction.

Lilly stood in the foyer, anger swelling inside her, an anger that had been building for the past three days. Without giving herself time to think or to change her mind, she stalked down the hallway and entered the office where Matthew sat behind a large oak desk.

"I need to talk to you," she said without preamble.

"I'm busy," he replied with the coolness in his voice that had been apparent for the past several days.

"Tough." She shut the door behind her, ignoring the narrowing of his smoke-gray eyes.

For a moment she wasn't sure what she'd come here to say. She gazed at him, taking in the sight of his wide shoulders beneath the white T-shirt, drinking in the careless tumble of his black hair, and fought the impulse to finger comb the silky strands into some semblance of order.

But more than that, she wanted to touch him on a mental level, somehow reach him in the depths of his soul.

"You told me that your father always punished you after Aunt Clara and I left here during those summers so long ago."

"And your point?"

She walked over to the desk, placed her hands on it and leaned toward him. "I'm just wondering why, now that your father is gone, you've decided you need to punish me and everyone else in the general vicinity?"

He averted his gaze from her and stood, keeping the desk between them. "Don't be ridiculous. I'm not punishing anyone for anything."

"Yes, you are," she countered. "And I have a feeling that for some reason you've been punishing your family for years."

She stepped back as he rounded the desk and came to stand directly in front of her. "You don't know anything about anything," he returned, his voice even-toned despite the ticking pulse in the side of his jaw.

Again she fought the impulse to reach out and touch him, stroke the jawline where the pulse ticked. "I know that eventually the anger you carry inside you is going to eat you alive."

"I'm not Danny. You don't have to worry about me swallowing a handful of pills or eating the end of a gun. I don't intend to kill myself, if that's what you're worried about." He jammed his hands into the pockets of his jeans, his eyes dark and his features set in grim lines.

"But don't you see, Matthew?" She gazed at him beseechingly. How she loved each and every one of his strong, bold features. How she loved the familiar scent of him that filled the air of the small office.

How she loved him, and that love filled her up inside.

"You are killing yourself," she continued softly. "You're just choosing to do it more slowly, less dramatically than Danny did."

His eyes narrowed once again and the tick in his jaw grew more pronounced. "I told you before, Lilly, don't counsel me."

"Then for God's sake, help yourself," she exclaimed with exasperation. "Your father was abusive. He was a hateful, angry man. But he is gone and you're an adult now. You aren't the only man in the world who had a bad father. Get over it, leave the past where it belongs...in the past."

She started to turn to leave, but was stopped as he reached out and grabbed her arm.

"Is that what you've done, Lilly? Put your past behind you?" His eyes glittered dangerously.

She raised her chin and met his gaze defiantly. "That's exactly what I've done."

"If that's true, then tell me why you're thirty-five years old and still alone. Tell me why you've decided not to get married, to have a family."

His demand caught her off guard, and for a moment she didn't know how to reply. "One thing has nothing to do with the other," she finally said.

For a long moment their gazes remained locked and Lilly felt a deep dark grief rip through her as she realized he was beyond her help, beyond her love.

He released his hold on her arm. "Why do you care, anyway? You keep nagging me to open myself up, stop keeping myself isolated from everyone. But you're going to run back to your own little safe, solitary life in Dallas. You aren't so different from me, Lilly. You've just fooled yourself into pretending that you are.''

His words created a renewed burst of anger inside her. This time it was she who grabbed hold of his arm, not wanting to give him a chance to back away from her.

''We are nothing alike,'' she said angrily, appalled by the tears that suddenly stung her eyes. ''You ignore your enormous capacity to love. You are so eaten up with the rage of your childhood, you can't get past it to open up your heart.''

She dropped her hand from his arm and stepped back from him. ''But I know I'm capable of loving because I've fallen in love with you.''

She wasn't sure who was more astonished by her words. She certainly hadn't intended to tell Matthew her feelings for him, and the shock on his face indicated he hadn't expected the confession.

''That's crazy,'' he said. For the second time since she'd walked into the office, he averted his gaze from hers. ''You're confusing good sex with love.''

''Don't demean it,'' she said softly. The sting of tears once again burned at her eyes. ''And don't tell me that I'm confused. I'm thirty-five years old, not some teenager besotted by my first sexual experience. I know what I feel and I'm not going to let you taint it or make a mockery of it.''

He stepped backward and raked a hand through

his hair, his eyes no longer emanating a dangerous anger but rather a tortured darkness.

"Lilly, I can't love you. I can't love anyone." His voice was thick with emotion. He drew a deep breath and moved back to stand behind the desk, as if he wanted the obstacle between them. "I'm sorry if I led you on...somehow gave you false expectations."

"You didn't." All she wanted to do was escape, run from the humiliation of spilling what was in her heart. "I just hope—" she swallowed hard against her tears "—I just hope you can eventually figure out the source of all your anger and get past it."

She turned and pulled open the door and left the office, tears now streaming down her cheeks. She raced upstairs for the privacy of her room, desperately needing some time alone.

Once there, she fell to the bed and wept tears of sadness, not so much for herself, but for him, for Matthew. If he continued on his path of isolation, he would never know the joy of love. He would never hear the sweet chords of a duet, know the unity of a couple, the completeness of a pair.

Then her tears became ones of self-pity. She wept because she knew he was right. She had carried the scars of her past for all these years, and it was those scars that had kept her alone.

He may have spent his life so far being angry, but she had spent hers being afraid. She'd been afraid to allow any man to get too close, afraid to open up her vulnerable heart. The abandonment by her parents had caused her to wrap her heart in protective layers.

Aunt Clara had wiggled beneath those layers and almost instantly Lilly had trusted that the woman wouldn't leave her, wouldn't cast her aside.

But Lilly had allowed nobody else close enough to hurt her, she hadn't allowed anyone close enough to abandon her. Matthew was right, in her own way she had been as damaged as he.

But what hurt the most, what ached so deep inside her was the knowledge that for him she would have been willing to take a chance.

Had he loved her, had he asked her to stay, she would have taken the risk. She sat up and swiped at her tears, her heart more heavy than it had ever been.

She had to face the fact that he didn't love her, that for him what they had shared had been good sex and perhaps some fun, but nothing more profound, nothing more heart shattering than that.

She had to face the fact that even though she wanted to believe that Matthew Delaney was her soul mate, the man she'd waited a lifetime to find, apparently she was wrong.

Matthew Delaney was a lone wolf and he intended to live a solitary life, and in that solitary life there was no room for her.

Chapter 12

She loved him.

Matthew sank down in the chair behind the desk, stunned by her unexpected revelation. Despite the fact that he'd been mean and cold to her, had tried desperately to keep her at arm's length, she loved him.

The knowledge ached in his heart with a pain that nearly stole his breath away. Surely she was mistaken about her feelings for him. Surely she knew better than to fall in love with him.

''Oh, Lilly,'' he breathed softly, and buried his face in his hands.

Somehow things with her had careened out of control. He should never have slept with her, should never have sought out her company. But his desire for her had been greater than his common sense. His desire for her had been greater than anything else he'd ever felt in his entire life.

In the brief time she had been here, she'd brought laughter back into his life. He'd felt a strange peace whenever they'd spent time together. But he knew it was a false peace that could explode at any moment.

She'd said he'd been punishing her, but what she didn't understand, what he couldn't tell her, was that what he'd really been doing was protecting her.

He knew that getting too close to him was dangerous, and so when she'd ventured too close he'd tried to shove her away with coldness and temper. But she'd refused to be shoved away.

He raised his head as he heard the sound of his family arriving, but he didn't move from his position behind the desk. She'd also said that she thought he'd been punishing his family for years. The very idea was ridiculous. He loved his brothers and his sister.

He'd spent most of his life trying to protect them from their father. He'd been the perfect son, trying to make everything right in an attempt to keep the old man happy and off all their backs.

Liar, a small voice whispered in the back of his head. He frowned, wondering where that had come from. Why would he even think that he was somehow lying to himself?

He rarely consciously pulled up memories from those years so long ago, but now he leaned back and let his mind drift back over the past...over those horrible years that had been his youth.

From the earliest time he could remember until the day of Lilly's last visit when he'd turned eighteen, the days had been filled with terror and uncertainty. The last day of Lilly's last visit had also been the last time his father had attempted to hit him.

Adam had reared back his fist and Matthew had grabbed hold of it. "If you hit me, be prepared, I intend to hit you back," he'd told the stunned old man.

That had been the end of Matthew's physical abuse, however the mental abuse had continued until the day Adam had died.

He wasn't sure how long he sat there, lost in the disturbing images from the past, when a knock on the office door pulled him from his thoughts.

"Come in," he called.

Luke stuck his head in the door. "Hey, brother. We're all here and just waiting for you."

Matthew nodded. "I'll be right out."

As Luke disappeared from the doorway, Matthew tried to dispel the memories that still cascaded through his mind. He stood and swallowed against the bad taste those memories left in his mouth.

With Lilly's confession of love still ringing in his ears, in his heart, and the retrospection into his youth filling his head, he felt more vulnerable than he ever had in his entire life.

Ill at ease with the strangeness of his emotions, he entered the family room where his siblings and their spouses awaited him.

I have a feeling that for some reason you've been punishing your family for years. Lilly's words went around and around in his head, making him half dizzy as he tried to shut them out...shut them up.

"Ah, there he is, the head of the household himself," Johnna said, the usual edge in her voice as she spoke to him.

The image of her as a baby, crying so desolately on the day of their mother's funeral exploded in his brain. She had never known the woman who had given her birth, and for most of her childhood Matthew had yelled at her, trying to keep her in line, keep her safe from their father's rage.

He had been a tough big brother...a tough big brother to them all. He'd browbeaten them into silence when there had been temper tantrums or tears. He'd ordered them to pick up their rooms, do their chores, do whatever it took to keep peace in the household.

And now, facing them, he was struck by his intense love for them all. There had been no time, no luxury of shared laughter, of whispered secrets among the Delaney siblings. It had all been about survival.

He braced an arm and leaned against the fireplace, aware of his siblings' gazes on him. As always they were waiting for him to tell them the reason for the family meeting. They looked at him to lead the way.

Shoving desperately against the memories and the well of emotion that threatened to rise up and usurp him, he opened his mouth to speak. "I tried to keep you safe," he said to Johnna, horrifying himself, as that had not been what he'd intended to say at all.

She frowned in obvious confusion. "Excuse me? Did I miss something here?"

Emotion swelled inside Matthew...emotion that he'd always kept tamped down, shoved away. But now he couldn't tamp it down. It was too huge, all consuming and he sought the anger that had always kept him safe, but it refused to appear to rescue him.

"When we were young..." he finally said. He looked at his brothers, then back to Johnna. "I tried to keep all of you safe."

Johnna's husband, Jerrod, stood and looked at Abby and April. "Why don't we step outside and give them a few moments alone. I think maybe this is a discussion for them to have without us."

As they all left the room, Matthew went over to the bar and poured himself a drink, surprised to discover his hands trembling slightly.

He needed to get control of himself. He had never felt as out of control as he did at the moment. He took a deep swallow of scotch, felt the burn of the alcohol as it hit the pit of his stomach.

"You never talk about it," Johnna said softly. "You never talk about father and our childhood. You've always acted like nothing bad ever happened to any of us."

"Maybe that's because he was father's favorite," Luke replied. Matthew looked at him in surprise. "Oh, yeah," Luke continued, "the old man was always telling me that I was a loser and why couldn't I be more like you. Matthew does things right, why in the hell can't you, he'd say over and over again."

"And he told me I was a big nothing, and it was

too bad I couldn't be more like Luke,'' Mark added. They all looked at each other in surprise.

''Don't you all see, that was his way of dividing and conquering us,'' Johnna said. ''When I did something bad, he always told me that one of you ratted me out. He'd tell me that Matthew told him what I'd done or Mark or Luke. He made sure I knew one of my brothers was a tattletale. He wanted us to distrust one another.''

Matthew knew what she said was true. Adam Delaney had manipulated his children to be wary of one another, to never trust or depend on each other. But despite his best efforts, Adam Delaney had not been able to keep his children from loving one another.

Again Matthew was filled with love for his brothers and sister, a love tainted by another emotion—the heavy, killing burden of guilt.

There were things he needed to tell them, things that needed to be said, but they were thoughts and feelings that he'd kept inside for so long, he wasn't sure he could say them out loud.

He set his drink down on the bar and felt a suffocating pressure in his chest. Again he sought the anger that had always been his friend, his barrier from any other emotion, and again it remained hidden and refused to come to his aid.

He was aware of their gazes on him, looking at him expectantly. He drew a deep breath and swept a hand through his hair.

''I was the oldest,'' he began. ''I should have done something more to help us.'' Suddenly the anger returned, rich and bold as it flooded through his veins. "Dammit, I should have done something more." He slammed his fist down on the bar.

Johnna stood and walked over to him and placed a hand over his fist. Her hand was cool, and he wasn't sure if the trembling he felt was from her hand or his own. "And what would you have done?" she asked gently. "What could you have done?"

Matthew tightened his fist, his short nails biting into his palm as his anger grew to mammoth proportions. "I could have killed him."

"No, you couldn't have," Mark objected, and came to stand next to Matthew and Johnna. He faced Matthew eye-to-eye, but there was compassion...there was love in his eyes. "You don't have the capacity to kill in you. None of us does. Despite what father told us, despite the role model he provided for us, we're good people."

Something inside Matthew...something deep and hidden and ugly sprang to the surface and cracked open. To his horror tears blurred his vision as he stared first at Mark, then Johnna and finally Luke.

"But I'm not good," he said. He shoved past Mark and Johnna and went to stand at the opposite side of the room, needing to distance himself from them as a sudden realization filled his head and the resulting guilt ripped through his guts.

"I'm not good," he repeated, his voice half-hoarse with emotion. He swiped at his tears, embarrassed by them and stared at his siblings bleakly. "Until this moment I always believed that I tried to be the good son, the perfect son to protect all of you. But that's a lie I told myself. The truth is I was the good son, the perfect son to protect myself.'' The deep dark secret that had poisoned his soul spilled out of him.

He drew a deep breath and fought against the tears that burned at his eyes...tears of pain...tears of shame. ''When father was beating one of you, I felt bad...but I also felt relieved, relieved that he wasn't beating me.''

To his horror, a deep, wrenching sob tore through him. ''God, how you must all hate me.''

''Hate you?'' Luke walked over to him and stood before Matthew. ''Hate you for what? For being human? For feeling the same things we felt? Sorry, brother, I hate to disappoint you, but there's not an ounce of hatred in my heart for you.''

''Matthew, did you really think you were the only one of us who felt relief whenever father was beating one of the others?'' Johnna, too, moved closer to him, her gray eyes soft and filled with love.

''I can remember lying in my bed and listening to father beating Mark and I wanted it to go on forever because I knew when the sound of those smacks stopped, it meant father might come to find me next.'' She flashed a quick smile at Mark. ''Forgive me,'' she said.

Mark nodded. ''It's like we were at war,'' he said. ''Even though we were just kids, we were all in intensive self-survival modes.'' He raked a hand through his hair, his gaze lingering on Matthew. ''For God's sake, Matthew, forgive yourself for being human. The only monster in this house was the man who was our father.''

Matthew looked deep into Mark's eyes and saw no censure there, no resentment or negativity. He saw only the shine of brotherly love, and for the first time in his life, he reached out and pulled Mark to his chest for the hug they both had needed for a lifetime.

As he hugged Mark, Matthew saw the tears that streamed down Johnna's cheeks. Johnna, who had always seemed so strong, so capable, wept like a little girl. He released Mark and gestured for his baby sister to come into his arms.

''I needed you to love me, Matthew,'' she cried into his chest as he held her tight. ''But you were always so cold...so distant. I thought you hated me.''

''I never hated you,'' Matthew exclaimed. ''I've always loved you, Johnna. I've always loved all of you. But I've been so afraid that you blamed me for everything that happened when we were growing up.''

Then they were all hugging and crying, healing old wounds that had festered for far too long. Matthew was overwhelmed by joy.

The guilt he'd never known he'd harbored, the guilt that had been so black, so desolate in his heart was swept away by the love he felt for his siblings and the love that radiated back to him from them.

Matthew felt as if he'd been washed clean, and for the next few minutes they all talked about the past. They spoke of their worst memories and their best and began the process of exorcising the power of their father from their lives.

For the first time Matthew shared his memories of their mother with the siblings who had been too young to remember her.

"We should have had this talk a long time ago," Luke said.

"The good thing is we finally did," Johnna replied. "And it's a good beginning. Maybe we are a family after all," she said, swiping at the tears that had tracked down her cheeks. "Maybe, just maybe, in spite of father's attempts to the contrary, we're really going to become the loving family we all desperately want."

Matthew nodded, too overwhelmed to speak. He went back to the bar and picked up his drink once again and took a sip. Thank you, Lilly, he thought. Thank you for picking and prodding and forcing me to look inside myself. Thank you for making me see how important my family really is to me.

"So what's up with this meeting tonight? Is this why you called one?" Mark asked.

Matthew laughed. "Not hardly. I didn't have a clue that all this was going to tumble out of us tonight." He finished his drink and set the glass in the sink. "To be honest, I called the meeting so I could tell you all that I'd reached a decision. I had decided that when the ranch becomes officially ours, I was going to sell my share to whomever wanted to buy it."

"And is that still what you want?" Luke asked, his gaze intent on Matthew. "Because, I'll tell you right now I would like for this ranch to continue being a family ranch, and we aren't a family without you, Matthew.''

Again emotion swelled up inside Matthew, but before he could reply to Luke, the door to the family room flew open and Lilly ran inside.

"The stables are on fire!" she yelled.

There was a moment of stunned inactivity, then they all sprang into action, rushing for the door and out of the family room.

As they raced out of the house, Jerrod came out of the kitchen. "What's going on?" he asked.

"Fire!" Matthew exclaimed. "The stables are on fire."

As Matthew hit the front porch and saw the flames already licking at the night sky, fear coursed through him. In this arid climate, there was nothing worse than a fire raging out of control.

The sounds of the terrified horses trapped inside the burning building filled the air. "Mark, Luke, see if you can get inside and get the horses out," Matthew instructed. "April, call the fire department. Jerrod, help me with the hoses."

They all sprang into action. As Luke and Mark disappeared into the burning stable, Matthew grabbed one of the water hoses that were always ready for just this kind of emergency. He knew better than to depend on a breakneck appearance by the Inferno Fire Department, which consisted of one fire engine manned by a volunteer team.

He grabbed one of the large hoses as Jerrod

grabbed another and together the two men raced toward the fire with water gushing through the hoses.

Closer to the stable, the air was acrid with smoke and ash, and Matthew felt a stab of relief as horses shot out of the stable, running away with wild eyes and frantic whinnies.

The horses could be rounded up later, he thought. Another wild burst of relief fluttered through him as he saw both Luke and Mark run out of the flaming inferno.

He was vaguely aware of Lilly holding a third water hose and disappearing around the side of the stable out of his sight. He wanted to call her back, wanted to tell her to stay at the house where it was safe, but he also knew they needed the extra water dousing flames.

And there were flames. Bright, huge towers of flames and showers of deadly sparks lit the night sky and turned it black with soot and smoke.

Luke raced to Matthew's side, his face blackened with soot. "I'm going to get another hose and wet down the rest of the outbuildings," he said.

Matthew nodded. As he battled the conflagration, he wondered how it had started—if it was an accident, an act of God or another attack on the Delaney ranch.

It took them nearly an hour to get the flames put out. Exhausted and black-faced with soot, the men stood before the stable assessing the damage.

The women joined them, grim-faced as they looked at the building. "I called the fire department, but there was another fire in town," April said, breaking the silence. "That's why the fire department hasn't arrived yet. The dispatcher told me Sheriff Broder was at that scene and would be out here later."

Matthew nodded absently, staring at the scene before him.

Luke disappeared around the side of the stables and came back carrying two cans of gasoline. "They're empty," he said. "Any of you know where they came from?"

Matthew eyed the metal cans and shook his head. "All the fuel containers we use here on the ranch are plastic. Those aren't ours."

"Then I'd say this fire wasn't just a matter of somebody carelessly smoking a cigarette or tossing a match," Luke replied grimly.

"Looks like we'll be in the market for some carpentry work," Luke said. "The damage is mostly contained to the back wall. We should be able to salvage some of it."

Matthew nodded absently. He wasn't surprised by the fact that the fire was obviously purposely set.

"Where's Lilly?" Clara asked, a touch of alarm in her voice.

Matthew looked around.

"She wasn't with us," April said. "Last time I saw her she was carrying a hose around the side of the stable."

"I just walked around the building. She wasn't anywhere that I saw," Luke replied.

A stab of fear swept through Matthew as he looked around frantically. "Abby, would you mind going up and seeing if maybe she went to her room?'' he asked.

Luke's wife nodded, turned and hurried into the house. A moment later the window in Lilly's room opened and Abby stuck her head out. ''She's not up here. She's not anywhere in the house.''

Dread ripped through Matthew as he looked around once again. Where was Lilly?

''Maybe we should spread out and call for her,'' Mark suggested.

Immediately they all fanned out, crying Lilly's name. A cold chill gripped Matthew's heart with each minute that passed and there was no answering call to their cries, no sign of her anywhere.

Had the fire been a ruse? A distraction? He thought of the snake in her bedroom, the mysterious rose that had been left for her. Terror gripped him. Where was Lilly? Dear God, where in the hell was Lilly?

He'd done it! He moved a chair closer to the side of the bed where Lilly lay, her hands tied to the iron bed frame. She was his. All his.

He leaned forward and sniffed her hair, her face, her neck, loving the fresh, sweet scent of her. He wanted to touch her face, run his fingers across her soft, silky skin. But that could wait.

Leaning back in the chair, he congratulated himself.

Setting the fire had been a divine inspiration. The diversion the fire had caused was just what he'd needed to accomplish his goal.

And the fact that it had all been so easy simply assured him that he and Lilly truly were destined to be together forever. He'd watched the Delaneys all arriving for the family meeting and he'd sneaked into the stables, splashing gasoline along the wall.

His hands had trembled while he worked, trembled with need, with desperation. It had been three days since he'd seen Matthew and Lilly making love, three days since he'd realized he had to act before he lost her to the handsome cowboy.

But in those three days there had been no opportunity to get to Lilly. She'd stayed close to the house, and with the party decorating going on, there had always been somebody with her.

But as he'd set the match to the gasoline, seen the flames leap to life with a whoop, he'd had a good feeling that this was going to work.

He couldn't believe his luck when she'd walked around the side of the stables by herself, nobody else in sight.

He'd known it was a sign from heaven, that now was his chance to take what should have been his years ago. He'd approached her and tried to get her to come with him willingly.

As she had realized his intent, she had fought with him, and when she'd opened her mouth to scream, he'd sent an uppercut to her chin that had knocked her out cold.

He'd scooped her up in his arms and had carried her away from the burning stable, away from the people who had no right to her, and had placed her in his waiting truck.

The basement of his house had been ready for her for days. The narrow windows were covered so nobody could peek in, the floor had been scrubbed and the bed made with clean, pretty sheets.

On the nightstand next to the bed was a bouquet of flowers and on the walls were several pictures. He'd wanted the place nice for her. He'd even bought fluffy new towels for the nearby bathroom.

He leaned forward again, noting the faint blue bruise that was beginning to appear on her chin. He hoped he hadn't hit her too hard, hoped he hadn't broken anything.

"Lilly?" he whispered softly. How he loved the sound of her name on his lips. "Lilliana," he said, using her proper name. "Wake up, darling."

She didn't move. There was no eye fluttering, no change in her breathing, nothing to indicate that she was anything but unconscious.

He sat back in his chair, content to simply sit and look at her and wait. He knew that she was going to be angry initially, that it might take her a while to realize they belonged together.

But he was patient. He'd waited seventeen years to finally have her, and now she was his. He had all of eternity to make her understand.

"It's all right now, Lilly," he said softly. "You're safe here." Maybe she'd be hungry when she awakened. He was a great cook, but decided maybe soup would be best for her after being unconscious. "I'm going to go upstairs and make you some nice hot soup. I'll be right back."

He stopped at the foot of the stairs and looked

back at her, his heart swelling with the force of his love for her. He just hoped he could make her understand. He just hoped she would love him back. Because if she didn't he would get angry. And his anger wasn't a good thing. Sometimes his anger even scared him.

Chapter 13

"It's all right, Lilly. You're safe here."

The words penetrated the fog of darkness inside Lilly's head. The content of the words was apparently meant to soothe her, comfort her, but instead a wild panic surged up inside her before complete consciousness had taken hold.

As the darkness fell away, pain stabbed her jaw and she attempted to move her hand, wanting to touch the place that was so sore. A renewed sense of panic shot through her as she realized her hands were tied over her head.

With an effort she opened her eyes and gasped aloud. She was on a single bed, her hands tied to the iron bed frame behind her head.

What was happening? Where was she? Why was she here? How had she gotten here? She closed her eyes once again and tried to think, tried to find an-

swers to the questions that whirled around and
around in her head.

She remembered the scene with Matthew in his
office, the humiliation of telling him she loved him,
then going up to her room. She remembered crying
with the pain of loving him and knowing he would
never love her.

Then she'd gotten up and gone to her window and
peered out. Fire! She'd seen flames eating at the
stable and had raced down the stairs and into the
family room to tell the others.

She frowned, her chin throbbing, making thinking
difficult. Yes, she remembered the fire and she'd
grabbed a hose to help douse the flames. While Matthew and Jerrod had worked on the front of the
building, she had hurried to the side, thinking to
attack the fire from another direction.

Her mind seemed to draw a blank there. She had
a vague recollection of struggling with somebody,
recognizing she was in danger. But that was all she
could remember.

Whoever it was she'd struggled with at the stables
had apparently brought her here and trussed her up
like a calf. She pulled at the cord that bound her
hands to the bed frame, but the knots were tight and
the frame was sturdy. She tugged and yanked for
several minutes, then stopped, exhausted and frus-
trated with the lack of success.

Did the people back at the ranch realize she was
missing? Did Matthew know that she'd been kid-
napped? "Matthew." She whispered his name and
prayed that he was looking for her this very minute.

But where was she? If she didn't even know where she was, how did she expect the Delaneys to know?

A wave of hopelessness overwhelmed her and she felt the sting of tears at her eyes. She swallowed hard against them, knowing that crying would accomplish nothing. Tears trekking down her cheeks without the ability to swipe them away would drive her insane.

She couldn't cry. She had to think. She had to figure out where she was and why she was here.

Her heart pounded as she heard the sound of footsteps above her. Then she heard the creak of a door opening and footsteps on the stairs. She quickly closed her eyes once again, feigning unconsciousness in an effort to come up with some sort of plan.

"Ah, my sleeping beauty," a familiar voice said softly. Whose voice? She'd heard it before, but at the moment she couldn't place it. She kept her eyes closed, afraid to open them and let whomever it was who held her know she was conscious.

Something cold touched the side of her jaw and she jumped and her eyes snapped open. "Ned!" she gasped in shock. Ned Sayville. Bewilderment momentarily usurped her fear. Why would Ned bring her here and tie her up?

"Ah, Lilly. You're awake." He smiled at her and placed the hand towel he'd used to touch her face on the nightstand. "I was afraid maybe I hit you too hard. You've been unconscious for a while."

"Ned?" she repeated his name, trying to make sense of this. He acted as if it was perfectly normal that she was tied to a bed in his basement.

"I'm sorry I had to hit you. You know I'd never hurt you unless I absolutely had to." Again he smiled. "I've made you some soup." He gestured to the serving tray on the nightstand. "I thought maybe you might be hungry."

Hunger was the absolute last thing on her mind. "Why are you doing this?" she asked. "Why am I here?"

He leaned back in his chair, his gaze soft and gentle, and that only managed to frighten her more. "Because this is where you belong. With me." He leaned forward, his breath hot and fetid on her face. "You're my destiny, Lilly. You're my life...my love. I lost you once, but then I got a second chance to make it right, to make you mine."

He was insane. It wasn't the kind of madness that screamed out loud. He wasn't picking imaginary bugs off his skin or spouting nonsensical gibberish.

Ned's madness was much more dangerous than that, much more insidious because it was hidden beneath a mask of normalcy. But she heard it in his crazy words, saw it shining from the depths of his brown eyes.

"Ned, you've made a mistake. If you untie me and let me go now, I'll see that you get some help," she said beseechingly. "I won't press charges. You won't be in any trouble."

He grinned again, the guileless, innocent smile of a man sure of himself. "I knew you'd say that. I knew it was going to take some time to make you understand. But you see, I lost you before and I just can't take that chance again."

"What do you mean, you lost me before?" She tried to ignore the pounding pain in her jaw, the ice-cold fear that flooded her veins.

"Seventeen years ago."

Again confusion swept through Lilly. "I don't understand," she replied. "I don't know you, I didn't know you seventeen years ago."

He leaned back in the chair once again, his smile one of infinite patience. "But I knew you. The instant I saw you I knew you were the one I'd been waiting for, the one who could take away all my loneliness and make my life perfect."

He laughed. "I can see you still don't know where we met, so I'll give you a hint. The Taylors."

"The Taylors? But they were a foster family I stayed with," she said slowly, racking her memories for some explanation to what was happening now.

He nodded. "You were there thirteen days and six hours, then you ran away."

She stared at him for a long moment. The Taylors had had three foster children in their care at the time Lilly had been sent to them. There had been a young boy named Billy, a thirteen-year-old girl named Sarah and a seventeen-year-old boy named Edward.

"Edward?" she said hesitantly.

He nodded, obviously pleased. "Edward is my real name, but I like Ned better. When you ran away, I looked for you. I knew my life wouldn't be right without you, but I couldn't find you."

Lilly's head reeled and the pain in her jaw grew more pronounced as she struggled to put together all of the pieces. "How...how did you find me again?"

His face shone with joy. "It was fate. I was on my way home from work and decided to stop at a grocer's I'd never stopped at before. There I was in the meat aisle, getting ready to grab a pound of hamburger and there you were, picking up some chicken breasts."

He stood, as if the excitement of the memory made it impossible for him to sit still. "I couldn't believe my eyes. I recognized you instantly and knew fate was giving me a second chance. I followed you for the next several days. I found out where you lived, what your schedule was, how often you visited your aunt. Then when I saw your aunt's house for sale, I spoke to the real estate agent and found out you were bringing her here."

He paced back and forth at the foot of the bed. "I came out here a couple of days before you and your aunt. I knew I had to be ready for our reunion."

"Ned, please let me go. Please untie me," she begged.

He stopped pacing and smiled sadly. "I'm sorry, Lilly, but I can't do that. I've waited too long for this moment. I've waited too long for you."

Once again he moved to sit in the chair at the side of the bed. "You know, I tried to forget you, I really did. I found two women who sort of looked like you and I tried to love them the same way I love you, but I couldn't."

"So was it you who vandalized the guest cottages?" she asked.

"That's right, and I put the snake in your room,

too." He shook his head with a rueful grin. "That was sort of a gamble. I was hoping you'd see it before it actually had the chance to strike you. After I took it out of your room and left the rose in your bed, I thought you'd understand about me and you, but you didn't."

"And you fired the shots at us while we were at the creek?"

"I fired at him...Matthew. I saw the way he looked at you, and it wasn't right. You're mine, not his." His eyes narrowed and the pleasant expression on his face transformed to one of anger. "I wanted him dead, but I missed."

Thank God, Lilly thought. Thank God he had missed. Otherwise the man she loved would be dead. Remorse filled her up as she realized she was the cause of the misfortune that had haunted the ranch.

As she looked at Ned, she realized something was missing. "What happened to your necklace?" she asked, remembering the piece of jewelry she'd admired. And there was a vague memory of her fingers grasping that neck chain just before he'd hit her and knocked her out.

His hand shot up to his neck, and surprise widened his eyes. He jumped up out of his chair, his eyes glittering with a dangerous light. "You'd better hope it fell off in my truck," he said. "'Cause if it's lost I'm gonna be mad. And you won't like me when I'm angry. Bad things happen whenever I get mad."

As he turned and hurried up the stairs, Lilly fought back a burst of hysterical sobs. She didn't know what to pray for—that she'd somehow managed to tear the chain off his neck and leave it on the ground outside the stable where somebody might find it, or that it would be in his truck and she wouldn't have to face Ned's wrath when he returned.

He returned a few minutes later, his face red with rage. He stalked over to the bed and slapped her hard enough that it made her ears ring and tears spring into her eyes. "You made me lose it," he exclaimed. "My mother bought that chain for me and now it's gone."

He drew several deep breaths, then sat in the chair next to the bed and reached out to gently touch her cheek. Lilly felt her skin crawl at his touch and fought the impulse to turn her head away.

"I'm sorry that you made me slap you," he said, then to her relief he removed his hand from her face and leaned back in the chair.

Despite the sting of the slap, a tenuous hope appeared in Lilly. Had she managed to pull the neck chain off and leave it on the ground at the ranch? Would somebody find it and come here to Ned's? Or had the necklace simply slipped off somewhere else, someplace where it would never be found?

She looked at the man who held her captive. What was he capable of? Would he rape her? The thought of him having sex with her made her want to throw up. Was he capable of killing her?

"Ned, you said that you found two women who looked like me and you tried to love them like you love me.'' She needed to know what he was capable of, what she was up against.

''That's right. Sarah was the first one. She worked in a bank and lived in an apartment not far from me in Dallas. I saw her on the street one day, and for a moment I thought it was you. But of course it wasn't. Still, I figured she'd be better than nothing so I started following her, checking out her schedule.''

''So what happened to her?'' Lilly asked in an effort to cut to the chase. She hoped he'd say nothing had come of it, that the woman named Sarah, who looked like her, was living happily in Dallas.

''To make a long story short, I started dating her and one night I talked her into coming to my place. That's when I tried to tell her that I thought fate had sent her to me as a replacement for you. She got all upset and tried to leave me and I got angry...so angry.''

He shook his head, a sad smile on his lips. ''She just wouldn't listen. That was the problem with Loretta, too. She didn't believe that she was mine and she made me angry. They're both resting in an old oil field just outside of Dallas.''

He'd killed them. Two women whose only crime had been they had a resemblance to her. Her heart ached for the two women, but the ache was tempered by fear, the fear that he had killed before so there was nothing to stop him from killing again.

Matthew was frantic. Nobody could find Lilly. They'd searched the house, then had gone to Aunt

Clara's cottage to see if she might be there. They'd checked everywhere they could think of, but she was nowhere to be found.

As he thought of all the things that had happened over the past couple of days—the snake in her room, the shots at the creek—his heart clenched with a kind of fear he had never known before.

He wondered if she'd been attacked and was now lying dead in the brush and that's why she'd been unable to return their calls. He shoved this thought away, unwilling to even think such a horrible thing.

As the others all gathered on the porch, unsure what to do next, Matthew walked around the side of the stable where he had last seen Lilly go.

''Where are you, Lilly?'' he muttered aloud as he slowly walked over the hard dirt. He knew better than to think she might have run away following their confrontation in the office. Lilly wouldn't have left the ranch without saying goodbye to Clara. Besides, her things were still in her room upstairs.

Something bad had happened to her. He knew it in his heart, he felt it in his soul. He spied the hose she'd been using, no longer sputtering water, but lying cast aside on the ground. She'd stood right here, and then what?

He gazed around, wishing the moon was just a little bigger, just a little brighter, to aid in the search for Lilly. Where in the hell could she be?

A feeling of imminent danger filled him as he continued to peruse the landscape before him. Had somebody come out of the nearby brush and dragged her away?

He squinted down to the dirt beneath his feet, looking for prints that might indicate where she had gone. Instead what his gaze caught was the sparkle of something in the grass nearby.

He walked over and leaned down. A piece of jewelry. He picked it up and stared at the cross with the roses crawling up it. His heart pounded. Where had he seen it before? On one of the ranch hands...but who?

Think, Matthew, think, he commanded himself. He closed his eyes and thought of each of his workers. Sayville. That was it. It belonged to Ned Sayville. So what was it doing here?

Ned. He'd been the one who had raced inside and saved Lilly from the snake. Had he played the hero to throw suspicion off himself?

Gripping it tightly in his fist, he ran back around to where the others were standing on the porch. "I found something," he said.

"What have you got?" Mark asked.

Matthew held out his hand, the gold piece shining in the porch light overhead. "It's Ned Sayville's." He swept past them all and ran down the hall toward his office. In there he had all the job applications, and on Ned's would be the man's address.

He reached the office and pulled out the thick manila folder that held the applications from the past year. Frantically he thumbed through them, seeking the one that would give him the address he sought.

"What are you doing, Matthew?"

He glanced up to see Mark in the doorway. "I'm finding Ned's address. I think he has Lilly."

Mark frowned. "What makes you think that?"

Matthew shook his head impatiently. "I don't have time to go into it." He found the application and quickly read the address—425 Briarcliff Road. He knew the area.

He grabbed a set of car keys from the desk then grabbed the gun from the drawer. "I'm going after her," he said.

"Are you sure Ned Sayville has her?" Mark asked. "He might have dropped that neck chain earlier today, or yesterday. There's no reason to believe he has anything to do with Lilly's disappearance."

"There's no reason to believe he doesn't have something to do with Lilly's disappearance." He hesitated a brief moment. "No, I'm not sure," he admitted. "But I've got to get to Sayville's place and check it out." He shoved past Mark.

"Wait," Mark replied. "You aren't about to go into this all alone. Those days are over. Luke and I are coming with you."

Matthew didn't wait. He felt the press of precious moments ticking by, and with each moment that passed he felt the thrum of danger increasing inside him.

As he got into his truck, he was vaguely aware of his brothers hopping into Luke's truck.

Matthew took off, not heeding speed limits, one single purpose in mind. Help Lilly. Save Lilly. The words reverberated around and around in his head. Help Lilly. Save Lilly.

Without her, Matthew might never have faced the killing guilt that had been inside of him for years.

Without her, he might never have talked to his siblings about their past, might never have found the peace and begun the healing that had begun this evening.

Love for Lilly welled up inside him. Although he'd tried to tell himself what he felt for her had nothing to do with love, he now knew he'd been fooling himself.

He loved her, thought he'd probably fallen in love with her years ago, when she'd been a charming, funny, sexy teenager.

He'd thought himself incapable of loving, had believed that his experience with his father had killed any soft caring that might have once existed inside him. But Lilly had nourished a seed of love that had been hidden deep inside his heart.

She'd made him realize that he could love, and the idea that she might never know what she'd done for him, that he might never be able to thank her was impossible to fathom. The idea that something bad might have happened to her ripped his insides into tormented shreds.

He didn't want to think about the possibility that he was wrong about Ned, that the neck chain had been dropped there yesterday, or the day before. If he was wrong about Lilly being with Ned Sayville, then all hope would be lost. He'd have no clue where else to look for her.

As they entered the town of Inferno, Matthew glanced in his rearview mirror. Luke's truck was right behind him, and he knew no matter what happened, no matter what they discovered, he could count on his brothers.

The thought of Luke and Mark joining forces with him to help Lilly warmed him. But the warmth couldn't compete with the chill of fear as he thought of Lilly.

He pulled to the curb two houses away from Ned Sayville's small ranch house. If Lilly was there, he didn't want to give the man any warning of their approach.

The others seemed to understand his intent and parked farther down the street. Matthew grabbed the gun from the seat next to him and got out of his car.

"Matthew..." Mark and Luke hurried to catch up with him.

"What's the plan?" Mark asked.

"Plan?" Matthew stared at them blankly.

"Before we do anything, we need to check out the house," Luke said. As if he sensed Matthew's impatience, he placed a hand on Matthew's arm. "We don't want to do anything that might make him hurt Lilly if he hasn't already."

A bleak wind of despair blew through Matthew's heart, but he nodded that he understood. "Looks like nobody is home," Luke observed as the three men stood at the curb, staring at the house before them. "His pickup isn't in the driveway."

Matthew pointed to a small, detached, window-less garage. "He's probably got it parked in there. I'm going to go around back and have a look."

Moving quickly but silently, Matthew rounded the corner of the house to the back where a patio was overgrown with weeds. There were no lights on back there, either, but as he moved closer to the house, he saw the small, narrow windows that indicated a basement.

Moving closer, he realized the basement windows weren't just dark because no lights were on, but something had been put in the windows to block any light from radiating out. Why would anyone put black paper or material over basement windows unless they were hiding something?

His heartbeat raced, and he knew with a certainty Lilly was in that basement. He just didn't know if she was all right or not.

Still moving as silently as possible, he returned to the front of the house where Luke and Mark stood guard watching the house.

"I think she's in there," Matthew said. "I think she's in the basement."

"So what are we going to do?" Mark asked.

"I'm going inside," Matthew said tersely as he tightened the grip on his gun. "And I don't intend to politely knock."

His two brothers nodded. "I reckon between the three of us we can get through that front door," Luke said.

Together the three of them approached the front door as quietly as possible. Luke reached for the doorknob and gave it a twist. "It's locked," he said, and stepped away from the door.

"On three," Matthew said. "One...two...three!" On the count, all three Delaney men hit the door with their shoulders. The force cracked the door frame and sprung the door open.

Matthew flew inside the house, vaguely aware of his brothers following close behind him.

Somebody turned on a light and Matthew looked for a door that would lead to the basement. He found it in the kitchen, threw open the door and half fell down the stairs in his haste.

When he reached the bottom step, the first thing he saw was Lilly tied to the bed. Myriad emotions roared through him. Relief and joy coupled with rage.

"Matthew, watch out. Behind you," Lilly cried.

Matthew swung around to see Ned Sayville charging him like an enraged bull. The man tackled Matthew, driving his head into the pit of his stomach and knocking him backward to the floor. The gun Matthew had been carrying flew from his hand and rattled across the floor, disappearing beneath a dresser.

"She's mine," Ned cried as he smashed his fist into Matthew's chin. "You can't have her. She belongs to me." Again his fist connected with Matthew's face, this time glancing off his cheek.

The rage that Matthew had always fought to contain exploded out of him like a wild animal finally set free. As he saw Ned's next blow coming, he twisted his head to evade the impact.

With the strength of his rage flooding through him, he rolled, pulling Ned from on top of him to the floor next to him.

As the two men grappled, each one seeking the

position of power on top, Matthew was vaguely aware of his brothers rushing to Lilly's side.

Ned fought with the strength of a madman, but Matthew fought with an equal, unrestrained force. The idea that this man might have harmed Lilly, might have laid his hands on her gave Matthew the edge of anger he needed for power.

With a roar he managed to gain the upper hand, and with Ned flat on his back on the floor, Matthew smashed his fist into Ned's face. Again and again he hit him, and someplace deep inside he knew he wasn't just hitting Ned Sayville, but he was also symbolically hitting back at his father, venting the lifetime of rage and hurt that he'd kept inside for so long.

For a brief moment he saw nothing but a curtain of red as he fell deeper and deeper into the festering anger. Then the curtain faded away and he saw the wounds that his fists had produced, knew if he continued, he'd kill the man.

He rolled off Ned and grabbed him by the front of his shirt and pulled him up from his prone position. "Luke, Mark, get this piece of dirt out of here," he said gruffly.

The two brothers each grabbed Ned's arms and half carried him like a limp rag doll up the stairs. Matthew rushed to Lilly, who stood next to the bed where she had been held captive.

"Are you all right?" he asked, wanting nothing more than to hold her in his arms, grab her against his chest and feel her heart beating reassuringly against his own.

But he didn't do that. He couldn't do it. He could love Lilly with all his heart. He could want her with every fiber of his being.

However, with the memory of that killing rage still burning in his head, with the vision of the red curtain of fury still burning in his eyes, he knew no matter how deeply he cared about Lilly, he would never have a life with her. He loved her too much for that.

Chapter 14

It was after one in the morning when Lilly and Matthew finally left the sheriff's office. Lilly had spent the past two hours telling the sheriff everything that had transpired from the time she'd stood at the side of the stable until they had broken in to save her.

It had been agonizing, reliving the fear that had filled her in that time she'd spent tied to the bed. But what was more agonizing was that she wanted desperately to be held by Matthew, only he wasn't offering his arms to her.

Now she sat next to him in his pickup traveling back to the ranch. Her jaw hurt, her arms burned with the muscle strain of being tied to the bed frame, but it was the ache in her heart that consumed her.

"I'm sorry about the stable," she said to break the uncomfortable silence that was thick in the air between them.

"Don't be sorry. It wasn't your fault." He shrugged and turned through the gates onto the Delaney property. "Besides, we can rebuild a stable."

He pulled up in front of the house, and Aunt Clara flew out the front door, tears streaming down her plump cheeks. "Oh, my sweet Lilly," she exclaimed, and pulled Lilly into her arms. "You poor dear. I've been so frantic."

For the first time since the horrid experience with Ned had begun, Lilly wept. She wept with residual fear, then with grateful relief. And she wept because the arms that held her, while loving ones, were not the ones she wanted most to hold her.

"I'll just leave you two alone," Matthew said as he started for the front door.

"Wait," Lilly said. "You can go ahead and lock up. I think I'll stay with Aunt Clara tonight." She knew she wouldn't be able to stand sleeping under the same roof as Matthew and not being in his bed, in his arms.

"Fine, then I'll see you in the morning." He walked up the front steps and disappeared into the house without a backward glance.

Again tears stung Lilly's eyes, and a sob caught in her throat. Aunt Clara placed an arm around her shoulder. "Come on, dear. You're safe now. Let's get to my cottage and get you to bed."

Lilly allowed the old woman to lead her to the cottage, where Clara gave her a nightgown to wear, then made up the sofa with sheets and a pillow.

When Lilly was settled on the sofa, Clara sat down in the rocker nearby. "Are you all right, sweetheart? Will you be able to sleep after the terrible trauma you suffered?''

Lilly forced a reassuring smile to her lips. ''Sure, I'm fine. Just tired.'' Although she had a feeling sleep would remain an elusive oblivion that she'd love to fall into.

She lay there a moment not speaking, instead coming to a decision. ''Aunt Clara, I think I'm going to leave in the morning and head back to Dallas,'' she said.

''Can you do that? I mean, won't the sheriff need you to be here so that man can be charged and put away?''

Lilly pulled the sheet up closer around her neck. ''According to what Sheriff Broder told me, before Ned can be tried for my kidnapping, it's possible he'll be extradited back to Texas to stand trial for the murder of two women.''

''Murder?'' Aunt Clara's voice squeaked in alarm. Although Lilly had called Aunt Clara from the sheriff's office to let her know she was all right, she hadn't told the older woman any details.

Quickly Lilly told her aunt what Ned had told her, about the two women apparently now buried in an old oil field. ''I was only able to give Sheriff Broder their first names, but he thinks that will be enough for the Texas authorities to begin an investigation.''

''We were so lucky,'' Clara said. ''We were so lucky that Matthew found that necklace on the ground and wasn't about to let anyone stop him from going to Ned's place.''

Lilly nodded.

"But the Halloween party is tomorrow night," Aunt Clara continued. "Wouldn't you like to stay for that."

Lilly shook her head. "I'm not much in the mood for a party. Besides, I need to get back home. I have a lot of things waiting for me there."

Clara was silent for a long moment. "Darling girl, you might be fooling yourself, but you aren't fooling me. I know good and well why you're going home. Because you're in love with Matthew."

Lilly started to sputter a protest, but Aunt Clara shushed her.

"A body would have to be blind not to see how you two feel about each other." Aunt Clara's chair squeaked as she rocked back and forth. "What I don't understand is why if you love him, you're running away?"

A lump filled Lilly's throat, a lump of tears that begged to be released. Instead of letting them go, she swallowed hard against them. "You're right," she said, finally managing to talk around the lump. "I love Matthew, but he doesn't love me."

"I don't know what would make you think such a thing. I've never seen a man so besotted with a woman like he is with you."

Her aunt was obviously seeing things that weren't there, Lilly thought with a wave of sorrow. "Matthew has no room in his life for anyone, and it's past time for me to get back to my life." She said the words with a note of finality.

Aunt Clara got out of the rocking chair and leaned down and kissed her on the forehead. "Whatever you decide to do, you know I'm behind you 100 percent. Now try to get some sleep. Everything always looks brighter in the light of the morning.''

Lilly murmured a good-night, knowing in her heart that nothing would look brighter in the morning. Until she could forget the love for Matthew that burned in her heart, until she could forget the taste of his sweet kisses, the magic of their lovemaking, she would know nothing but bleak emptiness, dark loneliness.

She'd thought that sleep would be difficult to find, but within minutes of Aunt Clara turning off the lights, Lilly slept.

She awakened just after dawn, the desire to leave Inferno and the ranch behind more intense than it had been the night before.

Aunt Clara was in relatively good health, the culprit responsible for the disasters at the ranch was behind bars, and there was no reason for her to remain here any longer.

She showered, then dressed in the same clothes she'd worn the night before. By the time she got out of the shower, Aunt Clara was up, and the scent of freshly brewed coffee filled the small confines of the kitchen.

She had a cup of coffee with her aunt, then the two women shared a heartfelt and loving goodbye. "You call me the minute you get into Dallas so I'll know you arrived safely," Aunt Clara said, hugging her fiercely.

"I promise," Lilly replied, then with a final hug

for the woman who was like a mother, Lilly headed for the main house.

It would take her only a half an hour or so to pack, then she could be on the road before eight…on the road back to the life she'd once believed so full but now realized was filled with emptiness, with loneliness.

Matthew wasn't in the house when she walked in. She knew he was gone by the absence of energy, the utter silence of the place.

She went up to her bedroom and began the task of packing. With every blouse she packed, with every pair of shorts she placed in the suitcase, a piece of her heart chipped off in despair.

When she was finished packing everything, she closed and locked the suitcase, then walked over to the window and stared out.

The stables she had once enjoyed looking at were now in shambles, half the building charred and burned. Like her heart. Burned by love, charred by sorrow. And she had a feeling the stables would be rebuilt long before her heart would be repaired.

She could have been happy here. She loved the ranch life, would have pitched in and done whatever needed to be done to assure the success of the ranch. But it wasn't destined to be.

With a deep sigh she turned away from the window and grabbed the suitcase from the bed. It was time to say goodbye, goodbye to the ranch she had come to love and to the man who would always possess more than a little bit of her heart.

She'd just reached the foyer when she met Matthew as he was coming in. His gaze swept down to the suitcase she held in her hand, then back up to her face.

''What are you doing?'' he asked.

She had hoped to leave without having to see him one last time. It would have been so much easier to sneak away like a thief in the night, taking with her the last of her dignity and the few pieces of her heart that hadn't shattered.

''I'm heading back home.'' She stepped past him and out onto the front porch, aware of his expression of surprise at her words.

''Do you think that's wise?'' he asked, following close at her heels. ''I mean, you had quite a trauma last night. Maybe you should just hang out here and rest for a couple of days.''

''That isn't necessary. I'm fine,'' she said, not looking at him. ''I just need to get back home.'' She stepped off the porch and headed toward her car.

''Lilly, wait!'' He ran after her, and she stopped by the side of her car and once again turned to face him. Why did he have to look so handsome, so wonderfully vital this morning?

Her fingers ached to touch his handsome face, her lips numbed with the need to kiss him, and instead of doing either she merely grasped her suitcase more firmly.

''What about the party tonight?'' His gaze held hers intently. ''Surely you want to stay for the festivities.'' He smiled, but the gesture looked forced and unnatural on his lips.

Even though she desperately wanted to return the

smile, hide the hurt deep within her heart, she couldn't summon anything like a smile to her mouth. "It's time for me to go. Besides, I'm not much in the partying mood." She opened the trunk of her car and placed the suitcase inside.

"Lilly, wait. Please. I need to talk to you." He swept a hand through his hair, his eyes beseeching her.

She stood hesitantly just outside the driver door. "What?" she asked with a touch of impatience. Every moment spent here was agony. Smelling his dear familiar scent, seeing his beloved face and knowing he would never, ever belong to her was sheer torment.

"I...I just wanted to thank you," he said.

The sweet beauty of his eyes would haunt her for years to come, she thought. Those smoke-gray depths that at the moment were soft and tender. "Thank me for what?"

A small smile curved one corner of his lips. "For picking and prodding at me and making me look deep inside myself." He took a step closer to her, and she leaned back against the car as her knees weakened.

"What are you talking about?" she asked. She wanted to tell him to get away, to stop looking at her so intently.

"Last night, for the first time ever, my brothers and my sister and I talked...really talked about our experience with my father. You were right. There was a lot of anger built up inside me, but last night I realized that I wasn't angry at anyone but myself."

He reached up a hand, as if to touch her hair, but then dropped his hand back to his side. "Something broke inside me, Lilly, and with the release of that poison came a love for my family and a peace I'd never felt before."

"I'm glad for you, Matthew," she said, speaking around the emotion that clamped tightly in her chest, threatened to spill from her eyes in the form of tears. She was glad for him, glad that he had managed to begin healing with his sister and brothers.

"Well, I need to get on the road." She fumbled in the bottom of her purse for her keys, fighting the flood of tears that begged to be released.

"It wouldn't have worked, Lilly," he said softly.

She looked up at him, surprised by his words. "Why not?" she asked, not even pretending not to know what he was talking about. If he truly didn't love her, he'd have to tell her now.

He averted his gaze from her as if finding it painful to look at her and speak the words he intended to say. She steeled herself for the pain to come.

"It wouldn't work because I have chosen to live my life alone." There was a deep, dark torment in his eyes, a torment Lilly desperately wanted to understand.

"Why? Tell me, Matthew. Make me understand."

He gazed at her, and in the depths of his gaze she saw something shining and bright, something that looked like love. A surge of hope filled her, but then dark shutters fell, obscuring the emotion she'd believed she'd seen there and dousing the momentary hope inside her.

"I can't explain it," he said, his voice deeper than usual. "All I can tell you is that I never plan to take a wife, never plan to live with any woman."

"Now tell me that you don't love me." Tears blurred her vision as she looked at him.

He jammed his hands in his pockets and once again averted his gaze from her. "It doesn't matter, does it? I've made my decision and that's that."

She drew a tremulous breath, any and all hope dashed. "Yes, then I guess that's that," she agreed softly. She opened her car door, a cold wind of desolation blowing through her. She slid behind the steering wheel and put her keys in the ignition.

He hadn't told her that it wouldn't work between them because he didn't love her. And there had been a moment as they'd stood looking at each other that she'd seen love in his eyes, felt love radiating from him. But it didn't matter now. Even if she wasn't mistaken and that's what he felt for her, he had no intention of following through on his emotions.

He stepped back from the car as she started the engine, her eyes filling with tears. I will not look at him again, she told herself. I will not look again at the man who held my heart but threw it away.

A sense of sheer panic suffused Matthew as he realized she was about to pull away. He knew she was crying, had seen the tears that had begun the moment she'd started her car. Her tears ached inside him, as did his love for her.

She'd wanted an explanation of why he couldn't allow that love to be the basis for a life together. And as he realized she was about to leave his life forever, he also realized she deserved to know the real reason he'd chosen a life alone.

He'd held her in his arms, kissed her lips with promise, made love to her in passion. He'd laughed with her and shared pieces of himself that he'd never shared with another person. She'd been loving and supportive, and she deserved better than what he'd just given her.

These thoughts whirled in his head in the space of a minute and suddenly he knew he had to stop her, tell her the secret he'd never told another soul. "Lilly," he whispered and reached into her open window and pulled the keys from the ignition.

"What are you doing?" she cried in obvious frustration. "Why did you stop me, Matthew? Just let me go," she said with a touch of anger.

He drew a final deep breath, then raised his head and looked at her. His heart constricted as he saw the trace of her tears, tears he had put on her face, in her heart.

He opened her car door and held out a hand to her. "I need to tell you something. I owe you an explanation."

"You don't owe me anything," she retorted with a touch of weary impatience.

"Please, Lilly. Step outside and let me talk to you before you leave."

For an agonizingly long moment he thought she

was going to deny him. Then she slid her slender hand into his and allowed him to pull her from behind the wheel.

Instantly she released his hand, closed the car door, then leaned against it, her arms crossed over her chest in a gesture of defensiveness.

Oh, how he wanted to draw her against him, stroke the shining darkness of her hair, kiss the lips that trembled with emotion. But he knew to do so would only make things more difficult for both of them.

"He beat her, Lilly." The words spilled out of him.

She frowned. "What are you talking about?"

Sorrow and pain welled up inside him. "My father. He beat my mother." He kicked at the ground and tried to swallow against all the emotions that rose up within him. "I don't think any of my brothers or sister remember that. They were too young. But I remember. I remember her pretty face all swollen and bruised. I remember her lip smashed and bleeding, her eyes black-and-blue."

Lilly's arms unfolded and she took a step toward him, but he stepped back, not wanting her to touch him, knowing that if she did, he'd crumble.

"I can't take that chance, Lilly. I love you too much, and I'm afraid I'm too much like him." This was his deepest, darkest fear, a fear he'd never spoken aloud, a fear he'd only examined in the darkest hours of the night. "And if I ever hurt you, I would die."

"Oh, Matthew." She had that soft, sweet look in

her eyes that made him want, that made him wish
for things he knew he could never have. "What on
earth makes you think that you're anything like your
father?"

She reached out and grabbed one of his hands,
and her touch was agony for him. He attempted to
pull his hand away, but she held tight. "When was
the last time you hurt somebody defenseless, somebody helpless?" she asked. "When was the last time
you allowed your anger to rage completely out of
control so you harmed another person?"

"Last night," he replied, and managed to pull his
hand from hers. He frowned as he remembered that
red curtain of rage that had descended upon him as
he'd hit Ned Sayville. "I...I lost control and gave
in to my anger, just like my father used to do."

"No," she protested vehemently, her eyes glittering brightly. "As far as I'm concerned, last night
you regained your control far too soon." She
touched the bruise on her chin. "I would have been
perfectly satisfied had you hit Ned another dozen
times. Your anger was justified last night, Matthew,
and that has nothing to do with you being like your
father."

She stepped closer to him, so close he could feel
her breath on his face, so close he felt a stir of desire
well up inside him. She reached out and placed a
hand on his cheek. He fought the impulse to close
his eyes and lean into her warm touch.

"You are not like your father, Matthew. I
couldn't love a man like him. And I love you so
much it hurts inside me."

Her words sent a deep torment through him, yet still he refused to consider anything else but letting her go. She leaned into him, her eyes shining bright, her body warm against his.

"Matthew, what your father did to your mother, what he did to you children, that had nothing to do with love. That was all about control and self-hatred. If you love me, if you really love me, then believe in that love…believe in yourself like I believe in you."

Her words wrapped around his heart and squeezed out the last bit of darkness, the last bit of cold despair. "Lilly." He breathed her name just before he gave her a kiss that contained every ounce of love, of tenderness and sweet desire he felt for her. And in the kiss she returned to him he felt the same things flowing from her.

When he broke the kiss, Lilly placed her hands on either side of his face, forcing him to look deep into the beautiful blue depths of her eyes. "You were right about me, Matthew. I have allowed my parents' abandonment to keep me alone until now, but I'm willing to take a chance on you and on our love. And if you let me drive away from here, then your father is still controlling you from the grave."

"I won't let you drive away from here," he whispered fervently. He pulled her back against him, loving the familiar contours of her body molding into his. "Oh, Lilly. I'm tired of being alone and I love you so much I can't imagine my life without you. But I've been so afraid, afraid that if I loved a woman, I'd hurt her like my father hurt my mother.''

''You don't have to be afraid of that, Matthew,'' she said softly. ''I know your heart, I know your soul, and you aren't capable of that. It's simply not in you.''

He closed his eyes, reveling in her words and finding inside himself the knowledge that he was not like his father, would never become like his father. ''Lilly, I love you so.''

When he gazed at her again, tears were once more shimmering in her eyes, but he knew those tears were ones of happiness, of joy. ''I have an idea,'' he said, his heart filled with love so intense it poured sweet warmth through him.

''And what's your idea?'' she asked.

''That we attend the Halloween party tonight together. But I won't go as a lone wolf. I'll go as a groom, and you go as my bride. Marry me, Lilly. Marry me and be my wife, fill my days and nights with love.''

''Yes, oh, yes, Matthew,'' she replied, and again their lips met in a kiss filled with the promise of a lifetime together.

When the kiss finally ended, she looked up at him, tears of happiness streaming down her cheeks. ''You know what I think?''

''What?'' he asked, and took a thumb and gently swiped at the tears, vowing that he would never, ever make her cry again with pain or unhappiness.

''I think fate brought us together as a reward for our miserable childhoods. I think our love and the life we're going to share together is a gift in exchange for the pain of the past.''

Matthew gazed into the sweet depths of her eyes and his heart swelled with the knowledge that she was right. She was his gift, one that he would treasure for all his days on earth and even into the hereafter. ''I love you, Lilly,'' he said as he once again gathered her into his arms.

''Then take me inside,'' she said softly. ''Take me into my home.''

''Home. Yes, with you there with me, it will finally be a home.'' As their lips met once again, Matthew realized he was no longer a man alone or a lonely man.

Rather he was the luckiest man in the world... because Lilly loved him.

Epilogue

"It's official." George Cahill looked up from the paperwork on his desk and grinned. "I am pleased to tell you all that you have met the terms of your father's will, and the ranch is now deeded to each of the four Delaney heirs and their spouses."

Matthew hugged Lilly closer to his side, a sense of pride welling up inside him. They were all there in the room, the people who over the past several months had become a real, loving family.

Luke stood next to Abby, his two stepchildren, Jessica and Jason, next to them. Jerrod and Johnna were arm in arm next to Luke and his family. Mark had an arm around a very pregnant April and his stepson, Brian, stood on the other side of him. Clara stood to one side, beaming happiness at each and every one of them.

The love that filled the room between the family

members wasn't the only positive thing that had happened in the past months. The stables had been rebuilt, the old barn renovations had been completed, and the ranch was enjoying a new financial success that was astonishing.

However, the most astonishing thing of all was the changes that had taken place in Matthew himself. The anger that had always been such a part of him had magically vanished, as if it couldn't sustain itself in the wake of the happiness, joy and love he'd found with Lilly.

Each and every day he awakened with Lilly in his arms and a prayer of gratitude on his lips. And each and every night he fell asleep with the same woman and the same prayer in his heart.

"Hot damn, we did it," Johnna exclaimed, and grinned at them all.

Suddenly they were all cheering and hugging one another. "Nobody could say it was easy," Matthew said when they'd all quieted once again. "We've battled outside forces from the very beginning, but the biggest wars were fought in the memories of our past and we've managed to win them as well."

"Could I say something?" April asked hesitantly.

"Of course, darling," Mark replied.

She smiled at Mark, a beatific smile. "You're going to be a father," she said, and touched her extended tummy.

"I know, sweetheart," he said, then grinned at his brothers.

"No, Mark. I mean right now," she said, and laughed with a touch of embarrassment. "I didn't want to spoil things, but I've been having contractions and they're now about two minutes apart.''

A look of sheer panic crossed Mark's features and he looked at first Matthew, then Luke. ''We've got to go,'' he said.

''Well, of course we do,'' Lilly said with a laugh. She walked over to April and gave her a quick hug. ''We'll follow you and Mark to the hospital.''

April nodded. ''We'd better hurry,'' she exclaimed.

Within minutes they were all in line, a caravan of family heading for the hospital. Matthew and Lilly took Brian with them, knowing Mark and April would probably go directly into the emergency room.

As Lilly, Brian and Matthew got out of his pickup, Lilly motioned toward Luke and Abby and their children. ''Brian, why don't you run ahead with Uncle Luke and Aunt Abby. I need to speak with your uncle Matthew for a minute alone.''

Brian nodded and hurried to catch up with Luke's family. ''Is something wrong?'' Matthew asked worriedly.

Lilly smiled, the warm beautiful smile he loved. ''What could possibly be wrong?'' she asked, and raised her arms to encircle his neck. ''A new generation of Delaneys is about to be born.''

''It's wonderful, isn't it?'' He wrapped his arms around her waist. ''My life is wonderful since I have you in it.''

''I'm glad you feel that way.'' Her eyes sparkled

with love. "Because in seven months I'm going to bring you back to this hospital."

Matthew stared at her. "What are you telling me?" he asked cautiously.

She laughed, the sweet sound ringing in the air, in his heart. "In seven months, Matthew Delaney, you're going to be a father."

"Oh, Lilly...sweet Lilly!" Tears of joy sprang to his eyes as he gazed at the woman who had filled his heart, filled his life with her love. "A baby! We're going to have a baby!" He whooped with excitement, then captured her lips with his.

"It's a whole new generation, Matthew," she said softly when the kiss had ended.

He stroked a finger down her cheek, his heart so full he felt as if he might die from happiness. "And this generation is going to be blessed," he said softly. "Because it's a generation born of love."

"Matthew!" Luke called from the door of the emergency room. "Come on, we need to all be together for this."

Together. The Delaney heirs all together, with their spouses and children, and the promise of a happily-ever-after for all.

"Matthew," Lilly said as they hurried toward the hospital door. "We won't tell anyone our news tonight. Tonight is Mark and April's time."

Her sweet thoughtfulness halted his forward progress, and he pulled her into his arms once again. "I love you, Mrs. Matthew Delaney."

"And I love you, Mr. Delaney," she returned,

that love shining from her eyes. "And you are going to be the most awesome father in the world."

He laughed exuberantly. "Ah, Lilly, does it get any better than this?"

Her smile held a sweet promise. "Darling, the best is yet to come."

As they entered the waiting room, where all the Delaneys were gathered, Matthew squeezed Lilly's hand, knowing the best was here and now, with the imprint of her kiss on his lips, the knowledge of their baby in his heart and the love of his family surrounding him.

* * * * *

Don't miss Carla Cassidy's next
Silhouette Romance in July!

INTIMATE MOMENTS™
presents:

Romancing the Crown

With the help of their powerful allies, the royal family of Montebello is determined to find their missing heir. But the search for the beloved prince is not without danger—or passion!

Available in June 2002:
ROYAL SPY
by Valerie Parv (IM #1154)

Gage Weston's mission: to uncover a traitor in the royal family. But once he set his sights on pretty Princess Nadia, he discovered his own desire might betray *him.* Now he was determined to discover the truth about the woman who had grabbed hold of his heart....

This exciting series continues throughout the year with these fabulous titles:

Available only from Silhouette Intimate Moments at your favorite retail outlet.

 Silhouette®
Where love comes alive™

Visit Silhouette at www.eHarlequin.com

SIMRC6

If you enjoyed what you just read,
then we've got an offer you can't resist!

Take 2 bestselling love stories FREE!
Plus get a FREE surprise gift!

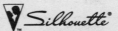

Where Texas society reigns supreme—and appearances are everything.

Coming in June 2002
Stroke of Fortune by Christine Rimmer

Millionaire rancher and eligible bachelor Flynt Carson struck a hole in one when his Sunday golf ritual at the Lone Star Country Club unveiled an abandoned baby girl. Flynt felt he had no business raising a child, and desperately needed the help of former flame Josie Lavender. Though this woman was too innocent for his tarnished soul, the love-struck nanny was determined to help him raise the mysterious baby—and what happened next was anyone's guess!

Available at your favorite retail outlet.

Where love comes alive™